Praise for Amanda

But I Love Him

"Ann and Connor inhabit every shade of hope, despair, confusion, ecstasy, longing, rage and guilt with heart-breaking realism … powerful and compulsively readable."

—*Kirkus Reviews*

"Beautifully written and wholly believable … This novel is a departure for Grace—who has written light, frothy tween novels under the name Mandy Hubbard—and marks her as a voice to watch in YA fiction."

—*Booklist*

"Intense. Scary. Heartbreaking. *But I Love Him* is a hard story to read, but one that needs to be told."

—*The Story Siren*

"*But I Love Him* is haunting, heartbreaking, and full of wondrous hope."

—*Sacramento Book Review*

In Too Deep

"Sam is a sympathetic character, struggling to define herself, and teens will empathize with her, even as she digs herself deeper into the lie. An ill-fated romance and tense pacing add to the appeal. Good fodder for discussion."

—*Booklist*

"*In Too Deep* is an easy, engrossing, uncomplicated but not oversimplified read that will be enjoyed by male and female readers who like reading about relationships and school culture."

—*VOYA*

The
Truth
About You
& Me

AMANDA GRACE

The Truth About You & Me

flux
®
Woodbury, Minnesota

First Edition
First Printing, 2013

Book design by Steffani Sawyer
Cover design by Ellen Lawson
Cover image of couple © Shutterstock.com/101311558/Aleshyn Andrei
iStockphoto.com/19247116/**Дмитрий Грибов**
Back Cover: iStockphoto.com/15552617/spxChrome

Library of Congress Cataloging-in-Publication Data
Grace, Amanda.
  The truth about you & me / Amanda Grace.—First edition.
      pages cm
  Summary: "Sixteen-year-old Madelyn Hawkins, who is taking college classes, enters a relationship with her biology professor, Bennett Cartwright, and knows she must keep her true age a secret from him. The story is told in the form of Madelyn's letters of love and apology to Bennett"—Provided by publisher.
  ISBN 978-0-7387-3624-2
 1. Teacher-student relationships—Fiction. I. Title. II. Title: Truth about you and me.
  PS3608.U2246T78 2013
  813'.6—dc23

                                        2013015753

Flux
Llewellyn Worldwide Ltd.
2143 Wooddale Drive
Woodbury, MN 55125-2989
www.fluxnow.com

Printed in the United States of America

For the kid's table—
Bree Ogden, Gordon Warnock,
Kristin Miller-Vincent, and Vickie Motter.
Because when we're together,
I finally feel like one of the cool kids.

Dear Bennett,

You might not read this, but maybe *they* will, and maybe somehow that will help you. This letter can't help *us*, because there is no us, not anymore.

Just saying that makes it hard to breathe.

I hope you *do* find it in yourself to read this letter, right down to the very last word, because maybe if you remember the way things unfolded—if you see it all through my eyes—you won't be able to hate me.

You never said you hated me, but I can't help but think maybe you do, because of what I did. What I made you believe.

I had to do it, though. I had to lie because I needed you, and if you'd known the truth, you never would have set the gears in motion, wouldn't have started something like two freight trains barreling down the tracks.

The crash was inevitable, because I wasn't who you thought I was.

I'm still two years from being who you thought I was.

Those falsehoods and half-truths started something that ruined you, and I know you can't forgive me, but I want you to remember me the right way, the *real* way it all happened, and not the ugly way they'll try to make it sound.

So for you, for me, for *them,* here it is:

The truth about you and me.

*

THAT DAY I walked into your classroom, I was a basket case of nerves. Maybe that's cliché, being nervous when starting a new school, but this wasn't just any new school.

It was college.

I felt like a kid, and the sad part of it all is that according to the police, I am one. So maybe I should have just listened to my gut. If I'd acted like I felt, you would have known the truth. You would have seen it coming a mile away, and you would have just fiddled with your Mac-Book and not met my gaze and smiled in that way that made your warm blue eyes crinkle up.

But I didn't act like I felt. I put my head up and my shoulders back and I walked through the door to your room. I'd been nervous before that moment, and when our eyes met, the butterflies turned to seagulls. I turned and walked to the back row so you wouldn't see me blushing. I found a seat next to a tall, pretty girl whose exotic dark eyes seemed sultry, sexy, without her even trying.

I'll never understand why you saw me at all, sitting next to a girl like that. I've spent my whole life being invisible because of girls like her. Girls who ooze the sort of sex appeal I can't even fake in my bathroom mirror.

But maybe the real world is different. I haven't seen enough of it to be sure. It sure seemed like it was different when we were together.

The class was Biology, but then you know that already. I guess I have to write some of this for *them*, too, so they know the truth. You'll just have to forgive me for saying things you already know.

Biology I was good at. Really good at. I didn't really enjoy it the way I enjoyed things like *Wuthering Heights* and Shakespeare, but it came as easy to me as brushing my teeth.

Math, too. You know I tested into Calculus, even though I'd never taken the prerequisite class? I skipped right over Pre-Cal. I think that's why my parents trusted me so much back then. It's easy to trust a smart girl.

Smart girls aren't supposed to do stupid things.

That day was beautiful, the late September sun filtering through those big evergreen trees, dappling the surface of my new desk as I plunked into my seat and pulled out a brand new spiral notebook. My mom wasn't so happy to discover that my school supplies and textbooks cost over three hundred dollars, but it's not like we had to pay tuition. Enumclaw High School paid that as part of the Running Start program. They paid for all of my classes at Green River Community College, and all I had to do was maintain a C average. I would get college credit and high school credit at the same time.

Maybe someone has explained all that to you by now. They probably mentioned it once before, too, but maybe you didn't pay attention, didn't give it a second thought. I bet you do now.

As I uncapped my pretty purple pen—something that seems so immature now—you stood up from your leather desk chair and walked to the center of the room, those long legs of yours making it just a few steps.

Right away, I liked the layout of your class—the desks were assembled like a horseshoe, so you could walk right into the center, so that we were all wrapped around you when you talked, smiled, gestured with those perfect hands of yours, just rough enough to seem masculine.

"Welcome to Biology 101," was what you said, and though there was nothing special about the words, the way you said them mattered. It was like you were telling us we were being invited into something extraordinary.

I don't know if it was love at first sight. Do you believe in that? Love at first sight? I wish I'd asked you this weeks ago, when I had the chance. I wish I'd asked you this days ago, when we were wrapped up in one another.

I probably won't get to ask you much of anything anymore, and maybe you wouldn't answer my questions even if I did. Maybe you have too many of your own.

You smiled as you handed out the syllabus, as you wrote your name on the whiteboard—*Mr. Cartwright*—in perfect, manly-but-not-ugly handwriting. It sounded British.

You look British, you know. Your face has that lean and rugged look, with the faintest line of stubble even at nine a.m., and your strong nose has the slightest bump in the middle, like maybe once upon a time some old chap in a pub punched you.

I know now that's not true, but that first day I imagined you sipping a pint of ale somewhere in the UK, wearing a sports coat with leather on the elbows. I guess that would have made more sense if you were an English professor. But you seemed worldly, and that's the image my mind made up for you.

To me, at sixteen, even the image of you sipping a frosty mug of Budweiser at the bar just outside campus seemed exotic. The guys at my school—my *high school*—were more likely to be found shoving one another out of the way in front of the Coke machine at McDonald's.

When the last syllabus slid in front of me—printed in pale green—I slipped it into my binder and then looked up again as you dimmed the lights and turned on your PowerPoint presentation.

As you had your head bent over your MacBook, the girl seated next to me leaned over. The faint smell of her perfume and hair spray washed over me.

"He's kinda cute," she whispered, her lips curling up in a devilish, confident sort of way.

I blushed, like she somehow knew I'd thought the same thing. "How old do you think he is?" I asked under my breath.

She studied you for a moment with her eyes narrowed, and I almost wished I hadn't asked, because I didn't want her watching you. I guess that's weird, that I already felt the tiniest twinge of possessiveness, but it's not so different from scoping out guys in the cafeteria. There's a girl code that says you can't go after a guy once a friend has a crush on him, and with you ... it wouldn't take much to get a crush.

"Twenty-four? Twenty-five maybe? But that seems kind of young, I guess ... "

And then you looked over at us, like you'd heard the whole thing but I know you couldn't have. She didn't seem to care that you'd caught us whispering, and you didn't say anything as your eyes swept over me and made me feel warm all over. Then you looked away and walked to the front and pulled down a big white screen, and the words *Cellular Composition* flashed across it.

"I'm Katie," she said, sticking her hand out. Her nails were cute—pale pink, but trimmed short.

I shook it. "Madelyn," I said.

"Pretty." She smiled and turned back to look at you. I wanted to tell her she was the pretty one, but I had a feeling she heard that a lot.

"Most of this unit is going to be a repeat of what you learned in high school Biology, but it's the building blocks for what comes next, so we'll talk about it as a refresher before we move on," you said.

But I didn't need a refresher. High school students take Biology as sophomores—for me, that was last year. For everyone else, it was more like three years ago.

You glanced back at the screen again and clicked that little remote in your hand, and a cell diagram popped up. And as you discussed the mitochondria and the nucleus, talking in an enthusiastic way with your hands motioning all over the place, it was poetry. Once or twice, you'd run a hand through that shaggy brown hair of yours, messing up the part so it was sort of rumpled but in a good, effortless kind of way.

You were right. Everything you talked about was familiar, and so I let myself daydream while you talked, watching your lips move but not listening to the words, and the two hours drifted by and you were closing your MacBook and I was shocked it was over so fast, that I'd gotten so lost in thought.

"Tomorrow will be our first lab day," you said. "In 3A, across the courtyard. See you all there at nine sharp."

Desks creaked, chairs screeched, and feet shuffled. Everyone else was halfway out the door before I even packed up my things, still blinking out of my stupor. I'd been thinking about a million things, none of them having to do with cell diagrams. Even Katie, her hips swinging, slipped out before I could say another word, her effortlessly stylish ballet flats slapping against the tiled floor.

I think it's because I was last to leave that you noticed me. Really looked at me, a smile tugging at one side of your mouth, a look so attractive it was hard to breathe.

"Everything sounding good so far?" you asked, adjusting the silver band of your watch as I strode toward the door. I blushed for a second, thinking you meant the sound of your voice, not the curriculum, before realizing I was being silly.

"Yeah, I think I'll manage." I paused at the door, and a long tangled strand of my wavy, dark-blond hair slid forward, off my shoulder. For a split second, your eyes followed it down before you looked back at your computer.

You stared at the apple symbol on your closed MacBook without blinking, and I wasn't totally sure what had just happened.

But I know now. I know you were scolding yourself for letting your eyes dip where they weren't supposed to go.

I know, when *they* read this, that maybe they'll think it means you planned everything, that you're attracted to underage girls. But I hope they remember that this was a community college campus, and so you thought I was eighteen or nineteen, like everyone else was.

You were annoyed with yourself because of that quarter-second glance at a student, because it was unprofessional.

Not because you thought I was underage. You didn't know.

You didn't know.

"Great," you said, your eyes still trained on that bitten apple. Did you think of the irony, then? That you were staring at the forbidden fruit to avoid looking at me? Because even though you thought I was eighteen, I was still forbidden. Students and professors aren't allowed to date.

I didn't know any of this then, not that day. I just thought you were embarrassed. But then you did glance up again, your eyes soft, warm, inviting. "I hope you enjoy my class, Miss … ?"

"Hawkins," I said. "But you can call me Madelyn."

"Well, in that case, you can call me Mr. Cartwright," you joked, your lips curling just enough to show that you had one funny tooth. Your smile was a little crooked. The whole thing was so at odds with your sophisticated flair, it caught me off-guard.

I laughed, and it wasn't a pretty laugh, either, but an ugly sort of bark of laughter, one I would cringe about for the rest of the day.

I stood a moment too long, so that it turned awkward and I realized you were waiting for me to leave, or at least ask a question. "Okay then, bye, Mr. Cartwright, see you tomorrow," I said, finally heading out the door just as the first few students from your next class slipped into the room, bringing with them the hum of voices.

"Yes, until then," you said.

I wanted to hear you say my name—just Madelyn, not Miss Hawkins—but that didn't happen until the second day.

It was just past noon when I got home. That's what was nice about Running Start—a full-time schedule was only three classes. Two of my classes were an hour long, five days a week, but Biology—my two-hour class—was only on Tuesdays, Wednesdays, and Thursdays. The rest of my friends were still sitting around at EHS, listening to the same old gossip, eating in the same old cafeteria, taking the same old classes. How could they be happy with that? How did they not feel like the ugly cinder-block walls were slowly closing in, like a coffin meant to trap them forever?

The house was empty because my parents work full time. My mom is an engineer at Boeing, and my dad is a Phys Ed teacher.

At Enumclaw High School.

He's not the sort of teacher people like, either, which never won me any points with my classmates. Dad, if for some reason you're reading this, I'm sorry to say that. It's not because you're not good at what you do. You are. You just expect a lot, and you're not the "cool" sort of teacher that students like. Even you must know we prefer teachers who are easy and fun, not the ones who are always pushing. Pushing is what you do, though. Who you are. You push your students just like you always push me.

To be fair, you only push as hard as you know you can. You just want everyone to live up to their potential. I know that. You were right last year; Ben Phillips *was* lazy, and if it hadn't been for you, pushing him at tryouts, he never would have made the football team, which is what he'd always claimed to want but never quite managed to pull off.

At one point, before high school, I took it all as a challenge. Almost a passion, really—the pursuit of perfection, the pursuit of that hug, the reward, the knowledge I'd succeeded. I thrived on the validation I got from Dad, from Mom.

And that's why every report card of mine in the history of everdom has a glossy A next to *Every Single Class*. Even PE, Dad's domain, which was nearly impossible to pull off since I inherited Mom's athletic ability and not Dad's.

See, the thing is, somewhere along the line I realized that I'd climbed aboard a plane and watched it take off, and all I could do was sit there with my seat belt fastened, waiting for it to land at a predetermined destination. One I wasn't sure I wanted anymore.

At some point I decided I didn't want to be pushed. I didn't want to be perfect at everything, charting the exact course that leads to Harvard or MIT. Somehow I just wanted to stop completely—unbuckle my seat belt, and jump off the plane—but I wasn't sure if had a parachute, a safe landing.

And for Mom and Dad, backup plans were a must. You couldn't turn without a new place to go to. But the validation my mom and dad gave me for being perfect just wasn't enough anymore. The "good job" comments, the pats on the back ... they meant nothing.

That day, as I stared at the television, instead of feeling stifled and stuck, my mind spun with images of *you*, Bennett, smiling at me. I replayed that moment when your eyes dipped low, and even hours later, my cheeks flamed hot and I hoped with all my might that I hadn't imagined that moment, because it made me feel ... different. Alive. Desired.

At three o'clock I got off the couch and went to my room. I spread my books out on the floor, along with a few random print-outs from my classes, and then I sat down right in the middle of all of it.

Like clockwork, the garage door hummed. Then the back door opened and swished shut, and I listened as my father's sneakers strode across the aging hardwood floors, each board creaking as he passed.

I crossed my legs and leaned forward on my elbows, picking up the syllabus to your class and staring at it as if it held the meaning of life.

Dad stepped into my room, his shadow splashing across the floor, and I glanced up, feigning surprise. "Oh, hey," I said, setting the syllabus down. For effect, I yawned and stretched.

Dad smiled as his eyes swept over my books, playing his part to a T. "Getting ahead already?"

I nodded, deciding that rubbing my eyes would be too much, so instead I played with a strand of my hair, twisting it around my fingers, remembering all the times Mom had pinned it up into a perfect, sleek bun back when I'd danced ballet. "Yeah. Some of my classes will be pretty tough, I think."

"Nothing you can't handle," he said, his eyes snapping up to meet mine.

It wasn't a question, just a simple statement. He expected me to agree, to rise to the challenge, just like I always did, because he'd been there to see me climb aboard that airplane and buckle up. He'd watched my trajectory for years, and this was just another mile closer to my destination.

I'd never understood the phrase, "You can't see the forest for the trees." To me, it seemed more like you can't see the people standing right next to you if they've been there all along. Can't see the moment they change, the moment they want to be someone else, because you'll forever see them as the person they've been.

"I've got it," I said, sliding my legs out from under me so that I could lie on my stomach as I reached for my English text.

And then just as the script progressed to *exit stage left*, he creaked his way back to the kitchen to go make dinner.

Every day, Bennett, it went just like that. Every day, I did things just the right way. Living up to my potential. Challenging myself. *Thinking of the future.*

Blah, blah, blah. Day after frustrating day, I stayed in the airplane, staring straight ahead, wondering why I no longer wanted to go to the place that had once seemed so promising.

And that day, he never questioned my act because he only saw the person I'd been for years. The perfect, studious daughter I didn't want to be anymore. I was six the first time he told me I'd go to an Ivy League school, just like Mom. I was going to make smart choices, like her—not have lofty, idiotic goals that could shatter just like his kneecap, not have dreams that could be stolen away like his dream of the NFL draft.

I was going to chart a careful course and find success in a calculated way, or else I'd be cursed to a third-rate career as a football coach and PE teacher. Because to settle ... that was to fail.

See, Bennett, I was tired of all this. So tired.

I chose Running Start because I saw the freedom in it. I saw the hours to myself. I saw escaping to a campus where my father wasn't teaching in the B Gym.

And that night as I fell asleep, I saw you.

*

I HIT TRAFFIC on the way to school the next day, and I whipped into the parking lot with my heart racing, worried, not sure if there was such a thing as a tardy slip in college.

I was late, ten whole minutes, to my eight o'clock English 110 class. When I walked through the door, breathless, my professor was already at the front, talking about our first essay assignment. My face flamed hot as every student in the room looked up at me when the door squeaked open. I thought I'd be reprimanded, but I wasn't.

College really is different. It didn't take long for me to figure out that no one cares if you come and go. If you chew gum, or stare out the window, or never turn in a scrap of homework. The more I got to know the rules of community college, the more I realized that high school teachers are sort of babysitters, and at college there is no babysitting.

And I really liked the sound of that, liked the idea that maybe when no one was looking, I could become someone else.

When class finally ended, I slipped out the door, ahead of the rest of the students, not wanting to be late for my second course of the day.

It's funny how, on that day, I was so consumed by the clock. If I could have a superpower, I think I'd wish for the ability to speed up time. Do you wish that, now? Now, when so much is happening so slowly, and you must be just sitting there waiting and thinking and waiting to see what happens next, what's going to tumble down or be rebuilt?

If I had that power, I'd give it to you. You must need it more than me.

I strode across campus that morning, the dew sticking to my cute little black flats, pleased that I didn't have to pull out the map again to remember where I was going. The campus, sprawled across a hill, was surrounded by evergreens. I felt so adult, so in control, as I navigated my route, cutting between buildings to get to the lab. There would be no bell ringing out the next class period, no hall monitors looking for passes.

Lab 3A was empty when I walked in, or at least I thought so. But as I stepped past an open closet door, you turned into me, and we collided.

You reached out to grab my arms, and you held me up.

You touched me, to keep me from falling, and I was so close I could smell you, a clean, aspen-like cologne washing over me. Something so different from the Axe body spray favored by high school boys, that sort of burning, overwhelming smell that follows them around like a cloud. Yours was subtle, sophisticated.

"Madelyn!" you said, your strong hands gripping my arms.

I stared, wide-eyed, back at you as my cheeks flushed hot. I'd smashed right into you, like some dorky little high school girl who couldn't look where she was going.

"Sorry," I said, hoping my face wasn't nearly as red as it felt. And that's when my brain caught up with my ears and I realized you'd said "Madelyn," and it made me smile so wide I must have looked pretty crazy.

"No, it's my fault, I didn't realize it was nine already. I was just hanging up my jacket." You jutted your thumb over your shoulder at the closet behind you.

That day you didn't have a V-necked sweater over your button-down, and it was easier to see the line of you, the way that cotton hugged your body.

"I'm actually a little early," I said, to make you feel better.

I'd never been more happy to be early, to get this ser-endipitous moment when our bodies collided. That's how it was with us. One day we were two separate people and the next we collided, and neither of us stood a chance.

I wish I could tell you I regretted everything that happened after that.

I walked farther into that room, and instead of sitting in the back like I had the day before, I plunked down at a table right up front, so that when you sat down at a desk in the corner, we were just a few yards apart.

I wanted to say something else to you, something witty, but a couple of other students arrived then, two guys who were laughing as they stepped through the door.

It shattered whatever moment we could've had, whatever impression I could have made.

They took the table in the back and the room filled up, and then Katie sat down next to me, flashing her pretty, easy smile. "Hey, Madelyn," she said, tossing her backpack onto the table.

"Hey," I said, even though I was a thousand miles away.

No, I was twelve feet away, in that place I'd stood when you touched me.

"Cool if I sit here?" she asked, playing with the newly pink-streaked ends of her dark hair. How did she have time to add something so cute in the twenty-four hours since I'd seen her last? "I'm betting we'll need lab partners."

"Sure," I said, finally forcing myself back to the present. Katie looked cute that day, in figure-hugging jeans and a sweater that dipped low over her cleavage.

I wondered, then, if I'd look like her, act like her, in a couple more years. She seemed so comfortable in her skin, so casually confident. The girls in high school, the pretty ones … their confidence seemed forced, fragile, all smoke and mirrors.

But not with Katie. With Katie, I'd bet anything she felt confident right down to her core.

Katie kind of grimaced, then. "It's only fair to tell you I'm miserable at science."

"It's okay," I said. "I'm really good at it. I took Advanced Bio last year."

She brightened. "Really? What school did you go to? I went to Kentlake. We had to do it as sophomores and that seems like a million years ago. I barely squeaked by then, and whatever I learned has officially leaked out of my brain by now."

"Oh," I said, my voice kind of falling. "Uh, Enumclaw. We have Physical Science as sophomores and Biology as seniors, so the class just ended a few months ago."

It was my first out-and-out lie, and I'm not even sure why I said it. You weren't listening or anything. But I liked Katie, I guess. I liked her warm smiles and easy chattiness. I didn't want her to think I was too young to be worth her time.

"Huh. Weird," she said. "But I guess that makes it my lucky day!"

But it was my lucky day, because friends didn't come that easy to me, and yet that's exactly how it seemed with her. I really was different, in college. I was changing and evolving, even on that second day.

"Starburst?" she asked, fishing a piece out of the front pocket of her backpack.

You watched me unwrap it. You watched me put it in my mouth. And then you looked away from me and stood up.

"Okay, guys, before we start let's go over a few ground rules for safety in the lab. Rule number one," you said with an amused sort of lilt to your voice, "absolutely no food or drink."

Katie and I shared a look, and she shoved the still-wrapped candy she was clenching in her hand into her backpack.

I used my tongue to push the Starburst to the side of my mouth, and I'm not even sure why because you'd already seen it.

Why did you watch me eat that candy and not stop me, Bennett? Were you letting me get away with it, or were you being playful with me?

"Rule number two: there are no make-up labs. Missed labs are simply going to show up as zeros, and that's going to hurt your grade. If you miss a lecture day, you can read the textbook. If you miss a lab day, you miss the lab. Period."

You walked around the room, passing out little packets of stapled paper. You wore nice shoes that day: pretty brown leather ones, not quite boots, not quite loafers, but something between. I liked the way those steel-gray slacks brushed the soles.

You dressed so differently than the boys at my high school, boys who wore nothing but ripped jeans and faded T-shirts. You cared about the way you looked, and it showed.

Katie shuffled our packet in front of me, and I trained my eye on the paper as she leaned toward me. "Teachers should not be allowed to look that good," she said.

I giggled. "*Seriously,*" I whispered.

You returned to the front of the room, and your shaggy hair slid into your eyes as I looked up at you. "Today's lab is really quite simple, but it will provide you with the tools for future labs. We're working on the basics of any good experiment: maintaining an adequate control group, creating reasonable hypotheses, and so forth. Please read over the material and then get to work. If you have any questions, please do see me, either during the lab today or during my office hours, which are outlined on the class syllabus. Today they're noon to two," you said.

Katie and I leaned together so closely our heads nearly touched and she read the instructions out loud, quietly. "I can grab the beakers," I said when she was finished.

"Great. I'll get the food coloring."

We shoved our chairs back and walked to opposite ends of the room, me to a bay of drawers right next to that closet housing your coat.

In high school, boys wear letterman's jackets, or fleece pullovers, or North Face snow jackets if it's super cold. I wondered, as I fished out a cylinder and two beakers, what your coat looked like.

When I walked back to our table, you were standing there, asking Katie what our hypothesis was. She was stammering something about a rainbow, and when I approached, her eyes looked up at me, pleading.

"We're hypothesizing that each of the colors, combined with water, will boil at the same temperature," I said, brushing past you to take my seat. It was a silly lab. A high school lab. But it accomplished what you wanted from us.

"Good. Very good," you said, your eyes meeting mine in a way that made it feel like a spark zipped between us. "I'll leave you to it," you said, going to the next table.

It went like that for the rest of the morning, with you floating around the room, me always aware of precisely where you stood, who you talked to.

Although Katie didn't know a dang thing about science, she was a good partner. She did exactly what I told her to, and her handwriting was perfect. I trusted her with our log book and I explained the experiment as we went along, and when you caught me talking about the difference between the control group and the experimental group, comparing them to drug trials and sugar pills, you paused, smiling in that special way of yours.

I wish I could see that smile now.

I wonder if you even smile anymore.

✳

SATURDAY MORNING, YOU changed your routine, and for that reason, our paths crossed.

Do you think it was fate, Bennett? Do you believe in fate?

I do. The same way I believe in soul mates and love at first sight. I don't think you can believe in just one of those things. Seems to me you have to believe in all three.

I was leaning on the trunk of a gnarly, drooping cedar tree, trying to catch my breath. I was only halfway up Mt. Peak. You always called it Pinnacle Peak, remember? Because that's what it's called on the maps. But nobody from Enumclaw calls it that.

To the locals, it's just Mt. Peak. I guess that's a weird name, like a river named water.

In any case, I was looking down at my battered hiking boots, trying to calm my burning lungs, when I heard a dog barking. I glanced up as a gorgeous golden retriever bounded up the trail, his reddish-yellow fur waving in the wind, his long tongue lolling out the side of his mouth.

I'm not afraid of dogs or anything—you know how much I love that dog of yours—but when he jogged right over and put his paws up on my chest, nearly knocking me down, I was less than thrilled.

"No! Down!" you said, and when I glanced up, my heart stopped. Doesn't seem like a heart can beat when it's way down in your knees, anyway.

Your face was flushed and your long-sleeved T-shirt clung to your muscled frame, the faintest outline of sweat shadowing your shoulders. When you looked up and met my eyes, you'd been about to say sorry. But instead you smiled and said, "*Oh,* hey, Madelyn."

Like we knew each other, like we were friends. You stepped up close to me so you could snap a bright red leash onto your dog's collar as he danced around at my feet. I no longer cared that he'd left two muddy paw prints on my T-shirt, that he was stomping on my feet.

"Hi, Mr. Cartwright," I said, wondering if my ponytail was jacked up, if my face looked as good as yours when flushed with exertion or if I just looked sweaty and ugly.

"I think we can dispense with the formalities outside of class," you said, reaching out like we were just meeting for the first time. "It's Bennett."

You have a nice handshake, you know. A solid, firm grip.

In that moment, an intense desire washed over me. I wanted our hands to be clasped in a different way. I wanted to casually hold yours, our fingers interlaced, and I wanted you to want that too.

That's what I was thinking, anyway. I don't know what you thought as our skin touched, palm to palm. All the time we spent together, all those talks, and I never did ask you how you felt about the first time we'd really touched. Voluntarily, that is. The crash into each other in the lab hardly counted.

Your dog chose that moment to take off, yanking you away from me, and you sort of pulled me with you for a moment before releasing my hand.

That's how we came to be hiking together on that quiet, foggy morning. *They* might think it was something you planned, that you asked to see me outside of class, but it was pure serendipity.

Normally, Mt. Peak is busy, but maybe people didn't want to climb the mountain knowing that the town was shrouded in fog and the view would be obscured. We only passed two hikers that morning, and neither of them paid much attention to us.

I liked that, too. That neither of those hikers thought it was odd that we'd be together.

"So, come here often?" you asked in a cheesy voice, as you cracked a smile.

You have a great sense of humor. Maybe that's past tense. I don't know at this point.

"Yeah. Most Saturdays," I said. "I like the quiet of it. Before the rest of the world wakes up."

You looked at me then. *Really* looked. Your blue eyes have this way of seeming kind of intense, you know. Not in class, but when it was just me and you and you let your guard down, let me see who you really are. You're more flippant in public, but that quiet sincerity of yours took over when it was just me and you.

"I know what you mean," you said. "It's relaxing."

"Exactly." We'd been hiking a few minutes, and our breathing had grown labored. We were only halfway up the mountain, but I made up my mind I would keep up with your long strides. You're at least six inches taller than me, so it was no small feat (feet? Ha ha, get it?), but I couldn't stand the idea of falling behind like some silly kid left in the dust. "How about you? You come up here a lot?" I asked.

"I've been hiking it every weekend, but on the other side," you said, jutting your thumb over your shoulder.

"The road?"

"Yep. I didn't even know there was a trail on this side, until I was standing at the top last week and someone appeared on the opposite side, where the trail emerges."

"It's prettier," I said. "I've always preferred this way."

You nodded. "Yeah. I like this side better."

You were talking about the trail, but I imagined you meant something about me, too, like you enjoyed hiking together.

"Can I ask you a question?" you said.

"Sure."

You glanced over at me, still breathing hard. "My class seems easy for you. You were the first one done with that pop quiz. How'd you get to be so smart?"

I smiled and looked down at the trail, concentrating on putting one foot in front of the other. "I don't know. My dad's a PE teacher at Enumclaw High School. He's really driven, wants me to succeed. He's always been there if I needed help, and I knew what the expectations were. If that makes sense."

You blinked. "Wow, did that suck? That you went to school with your dad there?"

Two things occurred to me in that moment:

(1) I wanted nothing less than to talk about my father with you.

(2) You'd asked that question in past tense, because you assumed I had graduated. But it *was* past tense, Bennett. It still is. I was never going back to high school because I was in college. Maybe I didn't have a diploma yet—I won't for two more years—but I was in college, and that's what mattered.

That's why, when I answered, you have to know I wasn't lying to you. I know it was still a deception in every way that matters, but I liked the way you were talking to me. Like we were equals, just a boy and a girl on a hike.

They say we weren't just a boy and a girl but a man and a girl, and so they should know that when I responded, I led you to believe I'd graduated. It was the first of so many half-truths. Just remember, Bennett, that at this point I still never dreamed you'd come to care about me, that we'd really become something. I just wanted someone to talk to me like you did. Someone who didn't see me as the same old bookworm, too studious, the wet-blanket sort of girl, but instead could build a whole new picture of me based on what I told him.

That's what I wanted. To paint my own picture for once, instead of taking over the one my parents had so carefully outlined.

"It was kind of unfortunate," I said, laughing like it was no big deal. "I'm just glad that part of my life is over."

"I bet," you said.

"What's your dog's name?" I asked, desperate to change the subject as I watched him walk right into the trickling creek bordering that part of the trail, his paws squishing in the mud.

"Voldemort," you said, grinning at me in that special way of yours, the one that was crooked and perfect in the same instant.

I laughed, and you joined in, and the moment held a certain kind of glow.

"He chewed up my favorite pair of shoes the first day I brought him home, so I couldn't help it," you said. "I usually just call him Mort because, you know, I'm probably too old to have a dog named Voldemort."

"And how old is that, exactly?" I asked casually. My legs were burning by then, but I couldn't bear the idea that you'd think I was out of shape, unable to keep up.

"Older than you," you said.

Maybe in that moment you were trying to put that wall up between us, erase the easy camaraderie. Your tone hadn't been sharp, but your meaning was clear.

You were telling me you were too old for *me,* that if I saw you that way, I shouldn't, that I should reel it all back in now, stamp down any childish ideas I had.

But it was too late for that. I'd started falling for you the moment I'd lain eyes on you, even if I didn't know it that day on the mountain.

"Oh come on," I said, my legs burning with the exertion of our hike. "Give me a hint."

Your eyes sparkled as you looked over at me, like you were enjoying the easy back-and-forth of our conversation.

"Let's see. I'm told the most popular song the year I was born was 'La Bamba.'" You reached out and snapped off a twig as we passed a little bush, then you started stripping off the leaves, leaving them behind us like a trail of bread crumbs.

"You really are ancient," I said. "Isn't that song from, like, the Middle Ages?"

Your laughter was infectious. I hope I haven't taken that from you. I couldn't bear to know you don't laugh like that anymore.

"The '80s, thank you very much. What about you?"

"What about me?" I asked, staring at the trail again, realizing too late I'd opened a door I should have left alone. Why had I asked you how old you were when clearly that only shone a light on my own age?

"What song was popular when you were born?"

If I'd told you it was a song by Diddy, before he was P. Diddy, back when he was Puff Daddy, would you have known? Would you have known I was just a kid, that I wasn't worth your words and your smiles and your laughter?

So I waved my hand in the air and said, "I'm not sure exactly. But it has *got* to be better than 'La Bamba.'"

"Hey, some great music came out of the '80s," you said, your voice both playful and indignant.

"So did Pee Wee Herman." I shuddered in an exaggerated way.

"Oh please, like the '90s were better," you said, bumping your shoulder with mine. You knew I was born in the 1990s—knew I was younger than you—but I'm sure you were thinking of the other half of that decade, the early part.

I grinned at you and bumped back. "We *are* responsible for Nirvana," I said.

I looked it up when I got home that day. Kurt Cobain died before I was born, you know. Three *years* before I was born. I don't know why I brought up Nirvana at all. I don't even like them. But when people think of the 1990s and Seattle—Enumclaw being a suburb of Seattle—they can't not think of Nirvana.

So maybe in that moment, on that quiet mountain trail, I unknowingly planted the idea that I was older, that I was around when Nirvana was still together. If that was true, I'd be at least nineteen, and that would make everything that happened okay.

"And how can I possibly argue with that?" you said.

We were nearing the top by then, a place where the trail plateaus. Voldemort ran ahead, chasing a squirrel into the brush, and you let him go, turning to see the vista before us.

I'd been wrong about the fog. By the time we reached the top, it was little more than wisps hanging low over a few distant fields, clinging to the edges of the big red barns.

"This view never gets old," you said, your breathing still labored as we stared out at the sprawling dairy farms and green foothills. "I could see it every day and never get tired of it."

Did you know you can see my high school from the top of that mountain? I didn't point it out that day, for reasons that must be obvious now, but if you ever go hiking there again, look to the west. You'll see its tan buildings stretched out in the distance, where the green farmland meets the infinite blue sky.

"Yeah, it's gorgeous. I just wish we could see the mountain," I said. By "the mountain" I meant Mt. Rainier, of course.

You turned around and glanced back, but the higher elevations were still shrouded in gray clouds. On a clear day it's breathtaking, all craggy rock and snow-covered peaks, the kind of thing that sells on postcards all over Seattle. In Enumclaw, it's up close and personal. Zoomed-in.

Voldemort jogged out of the tree line then, and I reached down to scratch him behind the ears. He sat down, leaning into my leg, and this time I didn't cringe at the slobber and mud that was sure to adhere to my clothes, because if he was yours, how could I not adore him?

"He likes you," you said.

I smiled up at you, still patting the dog. "Golden retrievers like everyone," I said.

"Ahh, but he is no ordinary dog," you said, your blue eyes bright, alive in a way they weren't inside your classroom.

"Oh?"

"He's Lord Voldemort!"

I laughed and we headed back down the trail, which was much more leisurely then the strained hike up.

We fit together, me and you, like two pieces snapping into place.

Ten years isn't so much, you know. If I'd been twenty and you'd been thirty, would anyone have even cared? It seems cruel that four little years were so important, so life-changing.

It was only two that mattered, really. The difference between sixteen and eighteen.

The difference between love that can span a lifetime, and love that can never happen at all.

*

THAT AFTERNOON, I sat curled up on my bed, leaning against the wall, my fingers on the keyboard, typing your name into a little white box.

I liked the name "Bennett" the instant you said it. It suited you. It was aristocratic, and sophisticated, and it fit my image of you sipping tea or ale or some such drink in a foreign country.

I don't know why I was so immediately fascinated by you, but I was. I'm sure I'm not the only person in the history of the universe who has read so much between the lines, to believe something is growing and building even if it hasn't been acknowledged.

Like that website, Missed Connections, that's just filled with stories of guys and girls meeting and going separate ways and never forgetting each other, even if they'd never actually spoken. It's a beautiful sentiment, don't you think? That some lonely guy living in a big city thinks he met his soul mate even though he never spoke to her, and then she slipped through his fingers, so now he wants a second chance?

It would be nice to know if you believed in things like soul mates. Maybe if you do, we'll find our way back together again.

In any case, I wasn't on that site then. I was on Facebook, and I'd just found your page, and my heart went whoosh when your picture came up. It must have sounded like a baby's sonogram heartbeat, moving so fast like that.

"Bennett Cartwright" isn't such a common name, I guess, because it was so easy to find your page. You were wearing a T-shirt that hugged your muscled frame and your brown hair was shorter in the picture, not quite falling into your eyes like it does now.

You didn't look that much older than the seniors who'd just graduated last spring, when I was a sophomore. Like maybe life didn't span so far between us.

Your last status update?

New quarter has started. Let the shenanigans begin.

Does that strike you as a funny update, looking back? You were twenty-five. I know that now. Twenty-five and three-quarters when we met, because we celebrated your twenty-sixth birthday together. That seems young for a college professor.

I didn't know it then, but that year was to be your first as a full-time, full-year professor. The year prior, you'd done only a few classes, not a full load.

That day, when I stared at your Facebook page, I wanted to know what kind of shenanigans you thought would be in store. I wanted to be a part of them. By that point in my life, I'd never been a part of anything that could be described as a shenanigan. No pranks, no detention, not even so much as a week of being grounded.

I was So Very Perfect.

I scanned your page. It wasn't private, and I was able to see all kinds of pictures. I shouldn't tell you this, but I saved a few of them on my computer.

I guess it doesn't matter if I tell you that. Mom took my computer away a few days ago, which is why I have to handwrite all this. I'm sorry for my handwriting, by the way. I hate it. This letter looks like it was written as part of a first grader's alphabet handbook: upright and rounded where it's supposed to be, angled just right elsewhere.

Sterile.

But I'm pretty much on lockdown right now, without a phone or a computer or anything, so you're stuck with it.

That day, as I scanned your page, I found something I didn't even know I was looking for. I smiled and sank back into my bed, that one word ringing over and over in my head.

Single.

You were single.

You should know, Bennett, that I was happy. It wasn't because I thought we'd get together. I knew that couldn't happen. I didn't even expect you to want a girl like me, not like that anyway.

But I wanted you to be single the same way a little girl wants her pop star, boy-band idol to be single. It's not because she thinks she's going to marry him. It's because she can't stand to picture the boy she loves—even from afar—with another girl, loving on her in real life when all she has is her imagination.

I wanted you to be single because I thought it would just about ruin those two hours of class every day to think of you married. To think of you going home to a pretty, womanly wife, maybe your high school sweetheart, and knowing I was still *in* high school.

All I wanted was to talk with you, maybe build up some sweeping *Pride and Prejudice* love story for us.

All in my head, of course, but what else was there for me to do? In this house with all that homework and expectations and pressure? My parents loved me—I don't know if that's true anymore, after all this—but I wanted a different kind of love.

And so knowing you were single made it okay for me to fantasize about you asking me to stay after class. Made it okay to imagine kissing you.

I know you'll think that's a stupid thing to say. Because your marital status was never the important piece of information.

No, Bennett. The most important thing, according to you, according to *them*, is that I'm sixteen years old.

✳

I WISHED ALL weekend that your class was more than Tuesday-Wednesday-Thursday. I wished with all my heart it was five days a week.

When I walked into your classroom on Tuesday—five minutes early, of course—and you saw what I was wearing, your eyes dipped lower, like they did on that first day, but it was for a different reason.

You were looking at my chest because of the T-shirt I was wearing. Because I'd prowled the malls all day Sunday, after our little hike, and I was wearing a black shirt with *NIRVANA* splashed across it.

You grinned at me in that unabashed way of yours, in the way of a man who knows who he is, what he wants. "Well played," you said.

I smiled. "I was going to wear my Hammer pants, but they were in the wash."

You shook your head, fighting a smile and losing miserably.

You were back in your sweater-and-button-down-with-slacks ensemble, and I have to admit I really liked that. I liked it because the Bennett I'd met on the mountain, with the long-sleeved T-shirt and Nike warm-ups, was meant only for me. Katie and all of your other students only got Mr. Cartwright, the professor.

We had something no one knew about.

It wasn't that we were trying to keep secrets, it was just that they came naturally to us. We shared that hike and we came back that Tuesday and we both knew something had shifted, but neither of us spoke of it.

I hadn't told my mom about you when I returned home after the hike.

I didn't tell Katie about it while we sat together in class that day.

But I thought of it, over and over.

I felt like an adult with you, Bennett. Not like a lost girl with a pretty, perfect shell, but like an adult in control of her life, going after the things she wanted. I felt like I'd finally stepped into the cockpit and decided to chart my own course.

Do you see me differently, now that you know the truth? Do you think I'm just a kid … and a stupid one at that? Or do you still see the girl I was all along? The smart one who aced all your tests and made you laugh?

That day, you paced leisurely back and forth as you lectured, and on occasion you caught my eye. Only for a moment, but that moment, it mattered to me.

It mattered more than you knew.

✳

A COUPLE DAYS later, I had to drop by the high school for the first time since last spring. As I shoved open the double doors of the main hall, silence greeted me.

It was strange, walking the halls, hearing the dull thud of my footsteps on the worn carpet, listening to the clang of a distant locker slamming shut. The classroom doors around me stayed closed, classes in session. Beyond them was the low hum of voices.

It had only been a few months since sophomore year ended, but it felt like ages. Like I'd graduated years ago and was swinging by to say hello.

Silly, that feeling. I was still enrolled at EHS. I was still a student. And yet, as the always-effervescent Marina Reynolds, a girl I'd once feared, rounded the corner, her familiar piercing gaze roving over my outfit before she smirked, I didn't get the usual twinge. I didn't pull on the hem of my shirt and I didn't dart my eyes, hoping she wouldn't see me.

I had a secret, Bennett, a secret that would trump any of their high school trophies, cheerleader skirts, or prom dates. It was like a candle flickering inside, warming me, dashing out the darkness.

That's who you were to me. A glint of warmth in a world that had felt so cold, so empty … so damned meaningless.

I rounded the bend. The *Main Office* sign greeted me, and I slipped through the doors, heading down a corridor that would bring me to my high school counselor's office. I had to see her regularly to plan my coursework. Not every college class at GRCC counted toward the specific requirements of high school graduation, so she needed to review my plans, be sure I would enroll in the right classes for the upcoming winter quarter.

I guess it was just lucky that Biology counted toward my diploma. What if it had been Chemistry, Bennett? I never would have met you.

Wait, maybe that doesn't make it lucky, not for you. Maybe it was a stroke of doom.

Her office door was open, so I tapped on the fake oak veneer and she looked up from her blackberry, her frown twisting into a too-bright smile. "Madelyn! You're early."

It sounded like an accusation, like I'd interrupted something more important than the trajectory of the rest of my life.

"Sorry, should I come back?"

She shook her head, her dyed-red ringlets bouncing around her ears. "No, no, that's fine. Let me grab your file. Go ahead and take a seat."

I slunk in and sat down, a little too hard, on the chair across from her desk, the vinyl-covered padding hissing a bit to let out the air in between the cracks. She crossed the room and pulled open one of the black cabinets, her fingers sliding across the tabs until she found the folder holding the last few years of my life.

So much about me packed into that thin folder. So many report cards, PSAT scores, college brochures with sharpie marker circling the entrance requirements.

And yet so little of me was actually captured. The person packed into that folder was a stranger, a robot. A girl in a gilded cage who could smile on cue.

The girl that my family knew, the girl I could no longer identify with.

"Alrighty then, how did the first two weeks go? Any concerns?"

I shook my head. "No, the classes are good."

"Not too hard? I was a little worried about packing in the general ed courses right up front. Most students do an art course, or a computer one or something the first quarter. Ease into things." She paused, studying me over the rim of her stylish, electric-blue glasses. "You're sixteen, after all, taking classes with adults."

I didn't like the way she said that, like I wasn't an adult too. But she didn't know me. "Yeah, it's art I'm no good at," I said, smiling to keep away a frown. "I swear I can't even finger-paint. Also, PE. But I can handle Bio, Calc, and English."

"Well, okay then. At this rate you'll have all the core stuff out of the way quite quickly. If we plan it right, you can have your associate's degree by the time you get your high school diploma. You'll enter your first semester outside of high school as a college junior."

My smile turned a little tight. I could feel it, the way the corners of my mouth stiffened; it felt impossible to hold like that. It was a silly reaction, really, because she was only rehashing the things we'd already talked about, agreed to. I'd always intended to graduate high school with my two year associate's degree because that was what Dad wanted, what Mom expected. "Um, right, that's the plan," I said.

"Are you sure? Technically you only need seven credits a year, and you're set up for nine. At this rate, you'll have enough for your diploma by the time you're halfway through your senior year. But your dad ... "

I let go of my smile and simply nodded, pursing my lips. "He talked to you? I thought that wasn't allowed."

And suddenly she drew herself up to her full height. Well, her full sitting-down height, and considering she was a hair over five foot, it wasn't that impressive. "Of course, I didn't discuss specifics with him about what we talk about when you're in my office. This is a safe room, and you can tell me anything you want. You know that."

Like hell I know that.

What I did know was that, apparently, my dad had visited my high school counselor, asked her to encourage me to take more classes. Asked her to push me.

Push, Push, PUSH. When would it ever end? When could I just ... breathe?

"However, he is of course allowed to know which classes you're taking. He has to sign the enrollment paperwork, so that information is relevant to him." She stared down at the first quarter enrollment forms, where I could plainly see my father's scrawling signature. "So I felt no need to hide it, as he'd see it anyway."

"When did he visit?"

"What?" she asked, glancing up from the sheet.

"My dad. Was it five minutes ago? Maybe it was yesterday and then again this morning, to be sure you knew what was expected? To be sure you didn't screw it up, that you accomplished what he needed you to?"

Her only reaction was to flare her eyes a little bit, probably in reaction to my rising voice.

Get a grip, I told myself. "Sorry," I finally said, after the woman just kept blinking at me. "I just didn't think he'd talk to you. I don't really want to … " And then I let my voice trail off.

If I told her I didn't want to take nine courses this year—when my high school classmates had seven—it wouldn't matter. And worse yet, she'd go straight to my dad and tell him, and then my dad would arrive home and I'd listen to a forty-minute lecture on the importance of education, on how he'd spent his whole life wishing he'd pushed just a little bit harder, reached just a little bit further.

I don't understand why he can't just push himself. Why he can't be more than a high school PE teacher. Maybe if he had his *own* freaking aspirations, he'd stop pulling on my strings and notice I'm not smiling anymore, not enjoying this.

I haven't even had any real friends in years. *Years*. My best friend in the whole world moved away in seventh grade, and I've never really replaced her. There've been study friends and ballet friends and neighbors ... but God, I have no true friends. Not really.

And for once, if my dad would stop pushing, maybe I'd stop feeling like my every action was controlled by someone else, like my mind and arms and legs were being yanked up and down and around with strings.

"Never mind," I said, that same old feeling of hopelessness seeping in.

"Okay then," she said brightly, all too happy to dismiss my momentary freakout. "Let's talk about what you're going to take next quarter. The catalogs will be out soon, and courses fill quickly. We don't have to decide today, but we should start—"

"Math, science, history," I said automatically. "I need all three, and I might as well take the higher level math and science courses right after the introductory ones, so that it's all still fresh in my mind before I move on to other stuff. Just tell me which ones count toward the high school requirements."

"Are you sure you don't want something lighter this time? Photography, perhaps?"

It was all I could do not to laugh out loud. Photography. Yeah, I'd be super good at that. Lots of experience there, getting out in the world, creating art.

"No, I'll stick with ... "

What's expected of me.
What I have to do.
Who I'm meant to be.
Who they've planned for me to be.

"Can we decide this another day?" I asked, a strange sense of power washing over me.

And as she smiled at me, that candle flame grew, bending and licking, thawing something around my heart. Something that had nothing to do with you, Bennett.

Yet somehow it had everything to do with you.

*

THAT SATURDAY, I waited in my car for you at the foot of Mt. Peak. I arrived early because I didn't want to miss you.

They should know that. If I hadn't gone to the edge of town that day, hoping and wishing for another hike, you never would have taken the next step. Things would have stayed inside that classroom of yours, and your wall—made up by button-down shirts and V-neck sweaters, beakers and cylinders, the PowerPoint and the syllabus—would have stayed between us.

But it didn't, Bennett. Because you pulled up in that S-10 pickup, Voldemort tied up in the bed hopping up and down and barely able to contain his excitement.

You were just planning on a normal hike. A hike like a thousand others you'd probably taken. But I'd planned a hike like just *one* other I'd taken.

It's me who's responsible for us getting together that day. It was always me, giving us the opportunities, nurturing our relationship along. Is that manipulative, do you think? Looking back, it does kind of seem like it. It didn't feel like it at the time. It just felt like you were irresistible and I needed more.

I climbed out before you came to a stop, as if to act like I'd only just arrived. I pulled my coat out of the back seat, zipped it up, and proceeded to walk toward the trail head like I hadn't even noticed you.

Voldemort gave me my excuse. He barked and I turned to look at him, pretending to be surprised. Did it look real, Bennett? Did you buy my act?

Had you been hoping to see me, the way I'd wanted to see you?

All I wanted then was for us to keep sharing this secret, these hikes that were only for us.

Remember that. As I waited for you in the shadow of Mt. Peak, I still never dreamed we would become what we did. I just liked the way I felt around you, liked that for one moment in my existence, I didn't have to pretend to be someone I wasn't.

I suppose that's irony at its finest, that I got to be myself around someone who thought I was someone else entirely. But you should know that my age is the only thing I never shared with you. Everything else, that was real.

When you climbed out of your truck, you were wearing a hooded sweatshirt. It had a big Seahawks eagle on the front and the pull-strings had been removed. It was faded and fitted.

I still have that sweatshirt, you know. I forgot to take it off that morning you dropped me off and never looked back. I hope it's okay if I keep it. It's all I have left.

That and memories of you as we set out on the trail, Voldemort jumping and wiggling and bursting with excitement, kind of like the way my heart felt whenever you met my eyes.

"So, Madelyn," you said, as we rounded the first curve and entered the dappled shadows of the forest.

"So, Bennett," I said, tucking my hands into the pockets of my coat. You looked at me when I said that, a little bit of surprise in your eyes. I guess you forgot that you'd told me your first name.

"Big plans for the weekend?" you asked.

I shrugged. "Oh, you know, just a marathon of bad movies and junk food in between studying. I have this Biology teacher, see, and he's a slave driver. We have these really annoying worksheets..."

You laughed and pushed me playfully on the arm, and I giggled, so happy you'd done that, so happy you'd touched me again. Was it meant to be flirting, Bennett, or more of a playfulness between friends?

I suppose that's splitting hairs, though. Maybe you don't even know.

Then you rolled your eyes and asked, ignoring my barb, "What qualifies as a bad movie?"

"Anything from the '80s," I quipped.

And you laughed again and shook your head but you couldn't wipe the smile from that gorgeous face of yours. "I like you," you said.

It was a simple thing to say, a simple sentiment to feel—you probably liked a lot of things—but it changed my world.

Because it changed what I thought we could become. Those three simple words, and I wondered if maybe it *did* matter that you were single, it did matter that we were out hiking together, it did matter that you and I seemed to have something real between us.

That was the moment I decided, Bennett, that I wanted to be with you, and that even though there was one very good reason we couldn't be something, I could come up with one *million* reasons why we could.

I threw my hair over my shoulders in mock arrogance, smiled at you, and said, "I know, I'm impossible to resist." I could see that you liked confidence, and I wanted to be that girl, the girl who owned who she was, enjoyed it, played with her girly side. A girl I'd never tried to be anywhere else.

You have this look, Bennett, this very special glowing sort of look when you're trying to rein in your smile but aren't quite able. Your eyes sparkle and you look just plain beautiful.

The silence settled in as we hiked, and it was comfortable, but I wanted to talk more, I wanted to connect.

"What about you? Big plans for the weekend?" I asked.

"Labs," you said. "I have about three thousand labs to grade."

"There are only twenty-five students in your class," I pointed out.

"I have three classes," you said.

"It's a good thing you're a science instructor," I said.

"Why?"

"Because your math sucks." I grinned at you, feeling clever.

I'd never felt clever, you know. I always felt smart, yet somehow never clever, never witty. In high school I felt like one of twelve hundred students, every one of us lost and confused and unsure of ourselves in one way or another.

But you made me different. You made me smart and funny and daring.

"Fair enough," you said. You paused for a second to whistle at Voldemort because he'd raced too far ahead on the trail. He whirled around and tore back to us, and three feet shy of us, he turned again and jogged back up the trail.

I think Voldemort meant to say we were walking too slowly, but I didn't want to go any faster. I wanted that hike to go on and on and on.

If I had that superpower, the one that could speed up time, I would have used it that day to slow things down. That hike would have gone on for days and days.

"Do you hike a lot?" I asked, because I felt like my lungs were burning, on the edge of exploding, and you were only a little winded.

"Yeah. A few times a week, at least."

"Where else do you go?"

You glanced up at the sky, a shimmery blue between the trees. "My favorite is High Rock," you said.

"Where's that?" I asked.

"Mt. Rainier National Forest. Way out past Eatonville and Elbe."

"What do you like about it?"

We hit a switchback and the trail narrowed, and you paused so that I could walk in front of you. I wondered if you were watching me hike. The back of my neck prickled and I wished I had eyes in the back of my head because I wanted so much to know if you were watching me. I tried to make my hips swing like Katie's did but I don't know if it worked, and since I was hiking, it was really hard and just made me more breathless, so I gave up on that.

"It's hard to explain. I should take you some time," you said. "You'd love it."

I was so unbelievably overjoyed and surprised by your invitation that I lost all ability to speak. My jaw flapped open and shut and it's a good thing you were behind me and couldn't see me like that, looking like a fish out of water.

"Yeah, that'd be awesome," I said.

A few beats of silence stretched out between us and I wondered if you regretted asking me that, like you'd said it but figured I'd decline.

You told me later it had been reflex, something you'd said before you could check yourself, remembered that I wasn't a friend, not really, and that's why the silence stretched out. Because in that moment you realized you shouldn't have invited me.

You also realized you wanted to. I think maybe, for you, that was the moment you acknowledged you wanted something with me, too. Maybe not yet a relationship, maybe not what we became, but *something*.

I glanced back over my shoulder at you, a little bit of hurt squeezing in my chest because I knew, I just *knew*, you were going to say something else, like *But we can't do that, because I'm your professor*.

You didn't say that, though. You just said, "We'd have to go soon. Once the snow stacks up, it closes for the winter."

"Name the time," I said. "Because now you have me curious."

"We could go next weekend," you said, and part of it sounded a little more like a question than a statement. There was just the tiniest bit of hesitance in it, and I knew you still weren't quite sure what you were doing, even as the words came out. Sometimes, with us, it's like our hearts spoke for us and our brains weren't on board. "Instead of hiking Mt. Peak again," you added.

My heart sang, Bennett. It climbed out of my chest and soared right up that mountain.

I don't know what you felt in that moment. Excitement, worry, both? You had your career to think about, and you thought you were breaking the school's rule.

Or maybe the rule is only about dating, and hiking surely couldn't be considered that, right? Is that what you told yourself?

"That sounds fantastic. I'm in."

We chatted as we climbed the mountain, about nothing and everything. And when we got to the top, I was pretty sure that view was even prettier than it had been the week before.

✳

THE NEXT WEEK was agony. Did it feel that way for you?

Did you ever regret inviting me on that hike, Bennett? I don't mean now, when you know how it all ended up, because I know you must regret it now, but back then, when nothing but possibility stretched out before us.

Back when you thought I was eighteen, Bennett. Did you regret it then?

It would just about kill me to think that you regretted it, that you spent all of that week thinking up ways to get out of it, to cancel on me without making a big thing of it. Because that hike—the promise of it—got me through so much that week.

My brother came home that Monday. My Very Perfect Brother. Dad cooked his Very Famous Lasagne, and Mom actually left work early so we could have a Nice Family Dinner, like we did when I was little, when I was the Very Obedient Daughter. I guess maybe I still was that girl, since it's not like I ever made a misstep, ever did anything unexpected, ever colored outside the lines.

Until you, anyway.

Dad made me polish the silver because we had a "guest" coming, even though it was just Trevor. My Ivy League, over-achieving brother, who apparently was supposed to give a rip whether or not he ate with fine china.

Dad and Mom are So Very Proud of Trevor. Dad brags about him non-stop, while Mom talks to him about numbers and angles and whatever garbage they study in engineering. He's the exalted one, that one I am supposed to follow.

Remember how I told you I was good at math, at science? It's because of Mom. Me and Trevor, numbers just click with us. Good genes or something.

I never wanted to be what Trevor is, but Mom and Dad never saw that, because by the time I realized it they'd already settled on the idea, grown it up like an enormous beanstalk, and how could I chop it down? When I didn't know what other choice I'd even make? That's something a two-year-old does—throws a temper tantrum without knowing what they'd choose instead.

It's hard to know who you want to be when you don't want to be the only thing you're good at.

That was my life. Black and white. And I wanted color. But I knew I'd find myself majoring in something uninteresting—for me that would be engineering, or science, or something in which the path was well worn and easy to navigate.

That's what I thought of that day as I sat in the high backed chair and I stabbed at that spring-mix salad, the lettuce too bitter on my tongue, listening as Trevor talked about his internship at an engineering firm up in Seattle, watching as Dad beamed and Mom hovered, thinking of how I could never be who I wanted to be without disappointing them.

I thought going to Running Start, being in college at sixteen, would be enough to get them off my back, buy me time to figure out what I wanted. But in that moment I finally realized, with horrific HD clarity, that there would never be a break, would never be a time they just decided to step back and let me be me, meandering wherever my path might lead.

See, Bennett, the sad thing about expectations is that if you fail them—by an inch or a mile, it doesn't matter—you disappoint people. And my parents, they don't set the bar low. And my brother, he just kept right on raising it.

I wanted fun, the kind of fun I'd never had. The kind of life and adventure I dreamed you were having. I'd watched enough MTV to know that other teens partied, and cussed, and fell in love and out again. They screwed things up, and they somehow came back together again.

But I'd never experienced any of that.

You only had a handful of Facebook photos but I managed to create a whole world for myself in them, something much like what I figured everyone else had. I imagined playing football or rugby or whatever you were doing in your pictures, the sky a vibrant blue, your cheeks flushed as you wore a jersey with a big number twelve. I'd be terrible at it, of course, but you'd laugh and help me and it would be fun. It wouldn't be competitive, and no one would care if I fumbled.

And then I imagined myself traveling to Paris, the Eiffel Tower in the background, me in the foreground, pretending I was squishing it between my two hands just like you did. We'd be goofy tourists, avoiding all the educational stops my parents would expect.

And I imagined myself in five years, on a barstool next to you, casually holding a longneck bottle, that neon light glowing behind me.

Behind us.

As I listened to my brother talk and my mom murmur "mhmms" now and then to signal she was listening, I let my mind drift back to the mountain, and the memories of our conversation were all that really kept me awake in that moment.

Maybe I'd perfected the art of dreaming with my eyes wide open.

"How does it feel to be one-upped, Trevor?" Mom asked as she speared that piece of asparagus that had been evading her for the last two minutes.

"Huh?" Trevor sipped at his glass of ice water, meeting Mom's eyes, and I saw his ego flash and glimmer in that defensive sort of way it always did, his eyes so easily readable with his dark hair gelled like it was. Because to him, Mom's approval was everything. He'd climb Everest and jump over the moon just to impress her. A few hurdles were nothing.

"Madelyn's in college-level Calculus at sixteen. Didn't you just take that class a few quarters ago?"

"Oh," he said. "Last year sometime, yeah." And he blinked, just once, and I knew he didn't like what Mom just said, the insinuations behind it. She didn't push on purpose, like Dad did, and yet it was always interlaced with everything she said.

All I ever wanted was a big brother, someone to watch out for me and show me how I was supposed to live, but all I ever got was a rival. I'm four years younger than Trevor and we still got pitted against each other, stood right up and measured to see who was the favorite that day.

And I wish Mom hadn't done that, hadn't thrust my accomplishments at Trevor that way. Because I knew he'd just go right back to raising that bar higher, making it impossible for me to reach, which meant I'd always be second best.

Were you ever in a pressure cooker, Bennett? Did you ever feel like you'd run through the fun house trying to ignore those twenty different versions of yourself, some tall and thin and some warped and ugly, only to reach the end and realize that there was no escape route, just more mirrors, more versions of yourself?

You were my escape route. My doorway to another world, a reflection that looked more like the me I wanted to be than the one I was forced to be.

"We're really proud of Madelyn," Dad said, and his voice was kind of raspy or gravelly or whatever, just like always, part of the cigarette habit he thought us kids didn't know about. A vice he couldn't admit, because it didn't match his history as a college ball player, as PE teacher...it was completely at odds with the man he pretended to be.

That's how my family is, you know. Everyone has some secret vice.

My dad smokes and my mom drinks wine every night—just a single glass—but she drinks it out of a coffee mug like maybe we all won't think a thing about it.

It's only one glass, Bennett. Just one. I know because I got curious once and kept track of how much was left in the bottle. But her *hiding* it, her not wanting to admit to that one-glass-a-day habit...my dad hiding his cigarettes in his sock drawer...well, that's just how it is in my house.

You have to be perfect, and if you aren't, well, you better fake it pretty damn well.

I faked it really well, Bennett. Just like that first day after your class, when I spent all afternoon sitting on the couch, thinking of you, and yet my dad thought I was studying because I knew to crack open the books and spread out my worksheets the moment before he pulled into the garage.

So, that night with Trevor, I sat in the dining room chair and did my duty, and it was thinking of you that made it easier. Thinking of our upcoming hike, thinking of the place called High Rock, hoping it went up so high it would take us somewhere else and we'd never have to return.

See, my dad had his cigarettes and my mom had her wine, and me, well, I had you.

*

ON THURSDAY AT the end of class, I had to linger behind because we hadn't agreed on where we'd meet, but I couldn't talk about it in front of anyone else. It was the first day I had to really work to hide *us* from everyone else.

Katie was sort of gathering her stuff, holding her book to her chest as she paused, waiting for me. I waved my arm and said, "I gotta ask Mr. Cartwright a question about next week's test."

I'd gotten used to thinking of you as Bennett, and saying Mr. Cartwright felt weird on my tongue, but you know I had to do it.

Katie nodded and slipped out of the room, and then it was just us.

You didn't pretend to be fiddling with your laptop or papers or anything like that. You just looked up and grinned at me, and in that moment my worry whooshed right out, because that wasn't the face of a guy who wanted to cancel our plans.

"Hey you," you'd said, and I read so much between the lines, read a casual comfortable air about the words that put me at ease.

"Hey yourself," I said. "I just wanted to know where we were going to meet up."

"Why don't we just meet at Mt. Peak, and then you can ride with me? We need to go that general direction anyway."

"Great. Just one other question," I said, stepping up beside you.

Your eyes darted over my shoulder, to the windows, even though we were only as close as any student and teacher would stand. I took a tiny, almost imperceptible step backward, and you seemed to breathe again, and something about your reaction stung, just a little.

Did you think I was going to close the gap, Bennett? That I'd touch you or flirt with you right there in your classroom, in plain view of all those passersby?

I wouldn't have done that. I wanted it a secret in the same way you did. But I guess your nervousness was understandable, so I tried not to be bothered.

"What's that?" you asked.

"How do you like your coffee?"

YOUR TRUCK SMELLED like pine that day, an almost over-powering scent. You bought a new little tree air-freshener for me, didn't you, Bennett? I was afraid to ask, because if the answer was no I would have felt oh-so-stupid, but I knew the truth.

There was not a scrap of garbage or a fleck of dust in the cab. You're a tidy person—I knew that by the careful way you hung your coat in class, by the organized look of your messenger bag—but I could see you'd cleaned that truck for me. As we settled into the long drive to High Rock, I cracked my window so that piney scent wouldn't overwhelm us.

I knew we'd be gone much longer than my normal hikes took, so I told my parents I was going to the library at school to study for your test.

Funny, right? That I actually mentioned you by name and they didn't suspect a thing? The strangest sense of pleasure ... of spite, in a way ... had washed over me that morning as I stepped out of the house, knowing that I had a whole day to myself—that we had a whole day to *our*-selves—and my parents would never know, because going to the library to study fit their image of the Very Perfect Daughter.

I knew that as long as I was perfect on the outside it didn't matter how I felt on the inside, so I enjoyed that long drive to High Rock, watching as you sipped at the coffee I'd picked up for you, happy that you drank it right to the last drop.

We drove down twisting country roads, next to lakes and hills, under trees and over little bridges. The farther we got from school, from home, from life, the more the mood changed, became lighter, as a day of infinite possibility stretched out just like that winding pavement.

"Still liking my class?" you asked.

I grinned and looked over at you. "Some parts more than others," I said.

"And what's your favorite part?"

"You," I said, feeling brazen.

I think you blushed, just the tiniest bit of warmth in your cheeks—cheeks that looked more clean-shaven than on an average class day—and then you said, "I have to admit, my eleven o'clock class isn't quite the same."

"Oh?"

You nodded, your lips curling just a little bit. "I shouldn't say that, you know."

"But I want you to," I said.

"Sometimes I find it hard not to look at you a dozen times in those two hours. I'm going to get myself in trouble." The way you grinned, your eyes still trained on the road, revealed that one crooked tooth of yours. My mom would say it *adds character*; I just thought it made you look even hotter.

"I guess I'm lucky. I'm supposed to look *only* at you," I said.

You reached out and playfully poked my arm, and I poked you back, and we were both smiling and it was beautiful, wasn't it? Us just being a boy and a girl and saying what we were thinking?

It hurts so much to think how complicated this all got, when it started from such a beautiful place.

Past Elbe, down a skinny stretch of pavement, you put your blinker on and turned onto a gravel road. The further we got from reality the more I wished your truck had bench seats, because I wanted to slide over until our thighs touched. I wanted to see if you'd rest your hand on my knee, or maybe wrap your arm around my shoulders and let me lean into you.

Voldemort had been quiet, back there in the bed of the pickup, as we drove down the paved county roads, but now he perked up and started biting at the wind and whatever tree limbs he could reach. It was another couple of miles on that puddled road, and when you hit the really big bumps we'd fly almost out of our seats, and then we'd laugh.

Finally, you parked the truck, and I was so pleased to see there weren't any other cars there.

"Did you bring any gloves?" you asked as we climbed out. It was so much colder up there, in the mountains, than it had been back home. I found myself surprised by the bite in the air, but I knew once we got hiking it wouldn't be so bad.

"Uh, no," I said.

"I have an extra pair."

You slipped a backpack over your shoulders and then tossed me a set of those stretchy, black, one-size-fits-all gloves and I pulled them on, imagining you'd worn them before, so it was almost like we were holding hands. It seems so childish now, like a girl with her first crush, but I couldn't help the thoughts from forming.

And a moment later I didn't have to imagine it, because you grabbed my hand and said "Come on," pulling me over to the trail head.

You were different that day, less cautious—like it didn't matter that you were my teacher and I was your student.

You wouldn't have acted like that if you knew I was sixteen. That's what I was thinking as you held my hand. I was thinking that I was doing something I shouldn't and I was thinking I was betraying you and I was thinking you would never have to know and that I could have what I wanted, and maybe years later we would laugh about it.

I hope *they* know that. Know that everything you did, every step you took, every touch you made, it was because you thought I was eighteen.

You let my hand go when we got to the trail because there wasn't room to walk side by side, and we fell silent as we traipsed up the hillside.

It was steeper than Mt. Peak, harder for me to keep up the pace you set, and we stopped periodically, sitting down side-by-side on fallen logs. Voldemort would race over and bury his face in my lap, making me giggle, and you'd pat his head.

I wanted to lean into you when we took breaks. I wanted you to touch me.

But we weren't there yet. You were still holding back.

It must have taken close to two hours to reach the spot where the tree line fell away and a giant craggy rock slanted steeply upward in front of us. The whole hike was only a mile and a half, but the angle of it, the steepness of that mountain, it slowed us down, and that was okay with me.

"What is this?" I asked, my eyes following a steel cable along the surface of the rock. At the top stood a ramshackle shed.

"It's a surprise," you said.

I turned and looked at you with raised brows, but you looked so happy, so eager, your blue eyes sparkling like that, that I just turned and followed you.

There weren't any trees or shrubs or grass, just a big peak of the mountain made of exposed rock. It wasn't vertical, though—I could still walk up it with the help of the cable. As that little shack loomed closer, my curiosity grew, and your face took on this glow like you were about to share something special with me.

It was one of those times when twenty-five looked young.

You still had that worldly, sophisticated atmosphere about you, but when that glowing smile took over, I could see you in startling clarity as a high school student, as just another boy who would have sat beside me in class. And it made all the guilt of being sixteen, of keeping that secret, it made it melt away, made me think that I wasn't so far off, we weren't so far apart.

We made it to the top and I saw that it wasn't just a shack, but an old cabin complete with a porch. It was perched on the edge of the rock peak, just a dozen feet shy of the drop.

I was afraid to let go of the cable, but as I stood there, holding on, my heart stopped.

I could see everything from that spot. The whole world, Bennett.

Mt. Rainier and Mt. St. Helens.

Mt. Hood and Mt. Adams.

Four of the biggest peaks in the state of Washington, and I could see them from one spot in all their snow-capped glory, a stark contrast to the tree-topped mountains surrounding them.

Below us, the National Forest sprawled. Miles and miles and miles of green, rolling valleys and steep mountains, broken up only by the occasional lake or river.

It was breathtaking.

You were breathtaking.

"What is this place?" I finally managed to say.

You stepped up behind me, not needing to anchor yourself to the cabin like I did, and stood so close to me I felt safe enough to let go.

"A long time ago, it was built it for smoke-spotting. Forest fires, you know? It was built in the thirties. They had to use donkeys to get all the pieces up here, and then this old guy would stay for days and days in the summer, watching out for smoke and fire."

"That's incredible," I said.

It must have been magical, being up there for days on end. The smoke-spotter must have felt like the only person left on earth.

"Come on, there's more."

I couldn't imagine anything more spectacular than what you'd already shown me. You took my hand again, and squeezed it, and then led me up onto the porch. You unlatched the door and we stepped inside.

There wasn't much to it. Just a small desk and a bed with no blankets.

And a notebook.

You picked it up and gestured for me to follow you back out to the porch, and then we sat down on it, our feet dangling toward the rocks. I swung my legs back and forth as you settled down beside me, cracking open that simple spiral notebook.

"See, people come from all over the place to see this cabin, and they write down their names and a message."

You took a pen out of your backpack and handed it to me.

"Write something for both of us."

As you handed over that pen, it was symbolic. You were giving me the honor of recording our moment up there on top of the world.

I could have written our names separately, one on each line, but I didn't.

I wrote *Bennett & Madelyn*, right next to one another. And then I tapped the pen against the page a few times, trying to decide what sort of message I wanted to add.

Others had left all kinds of things, nice messages like *Halfway through seeing the world!* or *Wow! Worth the hike!* and stupid things like *420 forever*.

I wanted my words to mean something.

I settled for *An unforgettable moment*, because that was the closest I could come to what I felt, and then I closed the notebook and gave you your pen back.

You put the notebook back where it belonged, so that someone else could hike up and find it and leave their mark on the world, and then you sat back down and unzipped your bag.

You brought food and drinks, Bennett. Do you remember what we ate?

Peanut-butter and jelly never tasted so good.

You brought only one big bottle of water, and as we passed it back and forth, it felt like it meant something. I'd shared pop and water with friends a million times, but with you, I imagined it implied something, a certain sort of intimacy.

"I can't believe how gorgeous this is," I said. "I wish we could stay here forever."

You nodded. "I always wanted to see the sunset from this spot, but there's no way I could hike down in the dark, and it must be cold as hell up here at night."

I agreed, because even in the full sun and all zipped up and wearing gloves, the cold was permeating me. Maybe in July or August, it would be warmer, but we were in October now, three weeks into the fall quarter. I shivered, and you took that moment to reach out, put your arm around me, and squeeze.

You rubbed my back softly as we stared out at the soaring mountains and plunging valleys, at that view that could never be topped.

When I turned to look at you, we were sitting so close, and the air around us so magical—so damned magical—I did something.

I leaned in to kiss you.

You leaned toward me, too, and my heart climbed into my throat, afraid to believe this was really happening, and at the last second—the *last* possible second—you turned your head just slightly and pursed your eyes shut, as if anguished, and you said two tiny words:

"I can't."

They came out on a whisper, almost too soft to hear, and yet those two words ruined me, crushed my heart right into my spine.

You didn't get up, didn't push me away, though. You just rested your forehead against mine and looked me right in the eyes, and we were so close I thought that if we blinked at the same time, our eyelashes would touch.

All those hours spent dreaming of being this close to you and there we were, so close, and yet I knew it was still too far away.

"I'm sorry," you whispered. "But I can't do this."

I felt sick in that moment, like the air up there was too thin and there wasn't enough of it to support my heart.

We both turned and stared at the vista spread out before us. The silence hung all around, and I wished we were still touching, in more places than our arms, our thighs, our knees. I wanted to lean my temple against your shoulder and feel your arm around me, and it ached to know it would never happen.

And then finally you said, "Twelve weeks."

I blinked and looked at you, and said, "Twelve weeks what?"

"A quarter is twelve weeks," you said. "And we have nine left."

I blinked again. I wanted you to be saying what I thought you were, but I was afraid it was too good to be true. I was afraid you were really saying, "At least we only need to see each other for nine more weeks, and then we can forget all about it." If that was what you meant, I didn't think I could stand it.

"And?" is all I said. It was all I could manage around the lump in my throat, because I'd wanted so desperately to kiss you and I'd lost the chance.

"And on December 13th, when those nine weeks are up, I will kiss you." Your eyes bored into mine, with all the intensity of the wildfires that were once seen from that cabin. "But if I kiss you right now, I might never stop."

I couldn't seem to say anything to that, so I just leaned forward and laid my head against your shoulder. You put your arm around me, just like I'd wanted, and we looked back out at that pretty, sweeping, breathtaking view and I let my heartbeat return to normal.

You wanted me. You wanted me and you had to wait nine weeks.

I could wait nine weeks for you, because you'd told me everything I'd wanted to hear. Everything I *existed* for.

I hope, when they read this, they focus on this moment, the moment where you did the right thing with all the information you had.

Because you thought the only thing keeping us apart was your job, and you were willing to wait until that one thing wasn't there anymore. And that means if you'd known I was sixteen—that I'd *still be* sixteen in nine more weeks—none of this would have happened.

That's why this is all my fault, Bennett. That's why I can't understand how no one blames *me* for all this.

Because you're a good guy, and if you'd known what I was holding back, you would have held back too. You proved you could, that day up at High Rock.

You proved you were good enough.

And all I proved was that I would do anything to be with you.

✳

WHEW. I HAD to take a break from writing for a few hours. Hours in which I did little more than lie in my bed and stare outward, watching the streaks of rain streaming down my windows. I know you might be waiting on this letter—might *need* it. See, the thing is, as I write this, I don't know where you are for sure. My parents will hardly let me out of my room, let alone the house, and I'm desperate to know what's happening to you. That's why I'm writing as fast as I can.

But I had to take a break, because thinking of that day at High Rock nearly undid me. I had to stop, stare at the rain, and finally take a shower to clear my head, a shower so long that the water turned cold. Because that was the turning point. The point of no return, the moment when I looked at you and jumped off the cliff, knowing I could never go back, could never reel in my feelings for you.

I know this is all my fault, and it's hard for me to bear.

In any case, I'm ready to tell the rest. Because the day at High Rock was only the beginning of us, not the end, like I'd feared in that heart-pounding moment when you pulled away before we could kiss.

Our hike was on Saturday, and I spent the next morning staring at your Facebook page, hoping somehow you'd update it, allude to an amazing weekend. I lost count of how many times my fingers hovered over the *Add Friend* button.

I knew I couldn't do it. Knew we had to hide whatever we were becoming, but God I wanted some kind of contact with you and we still hadn't swapped phone numbers, so all I could do was wait out that agonizing day of dreaming and thinking and wishing I could see you.

I thought about sitting at the foot of Mt. Peak all day long just in hopes of catching a glimpse of you, but I knew you wouldn't go, knew that High Rock was your big hike of the weekend.

So, after Facebook stalking you, I just lay on my bed and stared upward at the silly posters I'd tacked to the ceiling before freshman year, day-dreaming of you and frowning at the immaturity of the boy band featured on the poster.

And after three hours, I could no longer stand looking at their six packs, at their silly fireman costumes. So I grabbed my computer chair and stood precariously on the turning, rolling thing, yanking out the pins and watching as the first poster fluttered to the floor. It made a satisfying whooshing noise as it hit the ground.

Then I rolled my chair right over top of it, crumpling it, and climbed back on, pulling down the next poster.

And then the next.

And then I went around the room and took down the dried-up homecoming corsage I'd received sophomore year, when I went with my lab partner and it was the most epically boring evening of my life. That was just *last year*.

And then I pulled down the little movie stubs dating back five years, back to when I saw *Cars 2* with my brother.

Cars 2, Bennett. It seems weird to think of it now, but it wasn't so long ago that I'd gone to an animated movie targeted at kids not that much younger than me.

I dashed out of my room, took the stairs two by two, fished a garbage bag out from under the sink, and returned. I stuffed all those silly childhood things into the bag, one shred at a time. I wasn't a kid anymore, and this room was like a museum to my childhood. It didn't match who I was becoming. Who I was with you.

Then I turned to my closet. I still had my hoodie from sixth grade camp, even though it barely fit me, shoved into the back somewhere. And my middle-school PE uniform. Three pairs of too-small sneakers, one set of them with pink glitter and light-ups. Yeah, I'd been too old for those even when Mom bought them for me, but the fact that they were still buried in my closet was somehow even more embarrassing than it had felt when I wore them.

By the time I was done, I was sweaty and dirty.

Sweaty and dirty and *free*. Free to become who I wanted to be when you were around. I still didn't know how to be that person, outside of my time with you, but somehow I had to figure it out.

I shuffled the boxes around on the new, more spacious closet shelves, but one of them slid over too far and tumbled to the ground, bursting open and revealing stacks of photos.

I groaned, sunk to my knees, and righted the box, reaching for the first stack of pictures. I paused, my fingers leaving oily smudges on the sheen of the top photo. It was of me and my brother, both of us squinting into the harsh light reflecting from the snow all around us. I was eight, my hair in two long braids over my shoulders, a stocking cap with one of those big fluffy balls on the top pulled low over my ears, my cheeks pink with the cold, or maybe it was from the exhilaration of sledding.

We were at the golf course and a sled was shooting behind us in a colorful blur of red and blue. My brother's arm was draped casually over my shoulder, his other hand fisted to teasingly punch me in the stomach, something he'd do in a goofy way, never for real.

I was about to put the picture back into the box when something else caught my attention and I leaned in farther, my finger sliding over the spot below his eye.

The spot where a dark cloud seemed to hang, grow.

I swallowed, blinking, staring.

And then a memory came rushing back:

Me, reaching the top of the hill, huffing and puffing, pulling my little pink saucer up behind me.

My brother, halfway up, following my path.

When I got to the top, two boys—probably sixteen, a full eight years older than me—pelted me with snowballs, one of them crashing straight into my face and exploding in my eye like a thousand tiny pinpricks.

I dropped to the ground in an instant, the string in my hands disappearing as my sled skidded down the hill behind me, and I burst into tears.

My brother, who had seemed so far behind me, was suddenly beside me, then past me, the snow crunching under his feet as he flew forward after the two boys, both of whom towered over him.

And one of whom punched him square in the eye, while the other laughed and told us we matched. Then they hopped onto their sleds and slid down the mountain, and the world fell silent again.

My brother sniffled, just once, before he returned to my side and pulled me to my feet.

"You okay?"

And as he hugged me, I knew I was okay, knew my brother would protect me against anything. Anyone. Just like when he read me a chapter of *Harry Potter* before bed because Mom was at yet another conference in yet another city and Dad didn't do the voices right. Just like the way he gave me his own lunch on the bus when I burst into tears because I'd realized I'd left mine at home on the counter.

I blinked away the memory and tucked the photo more carefully back into the box.

Trevor and I had been close. A long time ago. Now he was consumed with pleasing Mom and Dad, in that same way that had once been so important to me yet now seemed meaningless. He'd moved away and forgotten me.

It stung, once. Now I simply accepted it as fact.

Once all the photos were back in the box, I stood, shoving it back onto the shelf.

Then I stepped back and surveyed the room, and my lips curled up. It was better. Much better. A room that suited who I was now.

As I left my bedroom again, heading down the hall to the bathroom for a hot, relaxing shower, my brother left his room and we collided.

"Oh!" I jumped back. "I didn't know you were home."

He shrugged, moving to step past me.

"Wait. Why *are* you home?"

He glanced back at me just before turning to take the stairs. "I have a few more days before I start the internship.

I raised an eyebrow. "What kind of an Ivy League school allows a sophomore to bail on classes?"

He pulled his phone out, glanced at the time, and then shoved it back in his pocket. "It's a pilot internship program for engineering students. The directors are Harvard alums and teachers themselves, and it's aimed at getting students directly into jobs after graduation. Which is a big deal, thanks to the job market or whatever."

"Lucky you," I said.

"Yep. Anyway, I'm gonna go play ball. See ya!"

And then, like that, he was gone.

And now that I'd cleaned my room, I was going to focus on another transformation. One I was hoping would catch your notice.

*

On my way to class on Tuesday, the radio hummed though I was hardly listening. I'd get to see in you in a few hours—for the first time since I'd added bright blond streaks to my hair—and I couldn't wait, couldn't stop the butterflies from racing in circles in my stomach. I wanted you to notice me in a new way, wanted your eyes to sweep over me. I'd never been particularly fond of the ugly dishwater color of my hair, and yet I had never changed it.

Until now. Because you changed me on the inside, and now I couldn't help but want everything else to reflect that. We were something. We had something. And I couldn't wait to see you again so we could figure out just what that something was.

As I clicked on my blinker and turned into the big lot—the western lot surrounded by all those soaring old cedar trees—three words from the radio echoed in my ears:

"Age of consent."

I had no idea what they were talking about ... or why, in that moment, I reached out and turned the volume up.

A woman's voice blared across the speakers. "I don't care what you say, a sixteen-year-old and a forty-year-old is gross."

"But again," a guy responded, "the age of consent in that state is sixteen. It might be gross, but it's not illegal."

"Yeah ... but ... ew," she said. There was a pause, and I frowned as the woman continued. "Anyway, moving on," she said, "today's big story out of Atlanta: a college volley-ball player has become infected with a rare flesh eating—"

I furrowed my brow as I clicked the radio off, pulling into a parking space and putting the car into park.

Age of consent.

Those three words rattled around in my head for a minute, feeling like a muffled, distant noise, until a moment of clarity—and hope, like a balloon lifting me from fear, from worry—sprung forth.

What if it wasn't about being a legal adult... what if there was another age that mattered? What if the "age of consent" wasn't eighteen after all, but something else?

If that girl could be sixteen and be with a forty-year-old and it wasn't illegal...

I jerked my seat belt, yanking it so hard it snapped upward and the buckle slapped against the window with a big clang. I grabbed my backpack from the back seat and slung it over my shoulder as I slammed the car door behind me and scurried across the parking lot, my feet lighter than they'd been for days.

Why hadn't I thought to research it? Why hadn't I checked to see if it was legal for you and me to be together? I'd just assumed, somehow, that I had to be a legal adult—eighteen years old—or anything we'd do would be illegal.

But maybe your line of thinking was right. Maybe once you weren't my professor, and that non-fraternization policy didn't stand between us... maybe it would all be okay, maybe I could tell you the truth.

It was a ten-minute walk from the far flung edges of the parking lot to the library, but I don't remember any of it—not the winding concrete pathways and certainly not the dew-covered shrubs I must have brushed into, given that my sleeves and jeans were tinged with water by the time I slipped through the glass doors of the library, walked across the wide expanse of floor, and made my way up the curving staircase to where the computers were.

I was supposed be in English class in three and a half minutes, but I couldn't bring myself to care. It was like I was staring at my dream as it dangled low on the branch ... and I was about to find out if I was allowed to grab it.

I walked past the first several bays of computers and around the corner, to where things were quieter and only three students were at the dozen or more terminals.

I chose the computer farthest from the other students and plunked down in the chair, dropping my backpack on the floor and wiggling the mouse to bring up the login screen. My fingers trembled a bit as I typed, and I had to backspace and put in my correct password. After three attempts, I logged in and the computer booted up.

Glancing around again, I popped open the web browser, typing in *Washington State Age of Consent.* I scanned the results, clicking on the third link. My eyes roved the page, looking for the answer I so desperately sought, feeling my face flush as everything in me strained with hope and fear.

Sixteen.

That was the number that leapt from the screen. A one and a six sitting there, blaring back at me as if they were glittering in neon lights. In that moment, I think I could have floated, flown, across the room. Or at least exhibited superhuman strength, like lifting a car or something. We could be together. On December 13th, we could be together and you wouldn't be in trouble.

But then it all crashed down as I read the next few lines: *Except when the older person is in a position of power (teacher, coach, etc).*

Teacher.

Surely they meant a high school teacher, right? You were a college professor.

But no matter how many times I read it—over and over and over—it still came back the same. I was sixteen, the age of consent, but you were in a position of power. Of influence.

For a moment I felt my heart being pulled into a dark blender, realizing that the possibilities that had danced before me had disappeared. But then I sat upright.

You didn't want to kiss me until December 13th anyway. When the quarter was over. When you'd no longer *be* my professor.

Then you wouldn't be in trouble professionally or legally, because you would no longer be in a position of power in relation to me, and I was old enough to consent to our relationship.

We really could be together. Soon. In December. I wouldn't have to wait two years for it to all be okay.

And suddenly those two years—those almost-ten years—they didn't matter anymore, not in the strictest way.

I didn't know what you'd think, how you'd handle it, once you knew I was sixteen. That's what terrified me most. I could wait weeks to be with you, could wait until December 13th. And then it would only be a few months until my seventeenth birthday anyway, and seventeen sounded so much older.

But I'd have to tell you, that day in December—before we became something more, something tangible—because it had to be both of us making that leap.

Making the decision.

But if you didn't turn away that day, December 13th ... we could be together with nothing to stop us.

✱

I HUNG OUT in the library for another forty minutes, until my English class was over and it was time for Biology, because I was too hyped up to concentrate on anything but seeing you. I left for the classroom a little early, wanting a moment to catch you alone.

But when I stepped through the door, you weren't alone. Another staff member was standing beside you. A pretty brunette with thick, curly hair and a sophisticated pencil skirt paired with vibrant heels. As I made my way to my desk, my eyes still trained on you and the back of her head, you glanced up.

But when your eyes met mine you promptly turned away, like you weren't willing to be caught looking at me. I ignored that little needling feeling. I knew why you had to pretend not to see me, but some part of me wanted to march right over and stake my claim somehow, talk about that fantastic view we'd seen at High Rock. Something, anything, to prove to her that I was something to you.

Instead I sat and watched you nod, and as she turned her body slightly I got a better view of her pretty, pastel-pink lipstick as she spoke. She was so elegant, so pulled together, so mature.

I don't know what you were talking about, but moments later she jokingly punched your arm and you laughed, and then she was leaving. You finally glanced at me again and I raised an eyebrow, as if to say *what was that?* Before I realized I was acting stupid.

She was your colleague, and I was acting like some weirdly jealous girlfriend.

And then other students were arriving, filling the room with shuffling and talking, and there was no room for another moment between us. After the last student plunked into the last empty chair, you stood and walked to the front of the room.

"Right, then. Before we start on today's test, let's do a quick review session."

Test.

The word rang in my ears, over and over, as panic rose.

I'd spent all weekend thinking about today, about class, about seeing you. And not a single ounce of the weekend studying. *Not a single moment.* There were three tests in the quarter—two midterms and a final. Cumulatively, they were worth half our grade, with the other half being the labs.

"Who can tell me which part of the cell is known as the 'powerhouse'?" you asked, using air quotes. You glanced over at a tall, lanky guy who sat at the farthest end of the horseshoe, the one who had two dozen football jerseys if his daily wardrobe was any indication. "Mr. Johnson?"

Mr. Johnson sat up, the desk creaking. "Uh, the mitochondria?"

"Right. And where are the chromosomes found?" you asked, turning to look around the room, waiting for someone to chime in.

"The nucleus," someone called out.

You smiled then. In the glow of it, I forgot my panic. You liked teaching, enjoyed seeing the progress we made, like a proud dad or something. It wasn't about proving yourself or being competitive. It was a simple sort of joy in what you did, and I had to admire it. For my dad, mom, brother, it was all about being the best at something, about showing off. With you, it was a simple pleasure.

"Good. And the ribosomes?"

Your eyes roamed the room, waiting for someone to call it out, but there was only the rustling of paper, the scraping of chairs. And then your eyes landed on me and I smiled at you, remembering High Rock, remembering the feel of the sun on our cheeks even as the crisp air stole our heat away.

And then suddenly my cheeks warmed as I pushed the memory away, realizing the entire class was staring at me, including you.

"Uh, what?" I said, coughing to clear my throat. I had no idea what you'd asked me.

"The ribosomes. What are they for?"

My mouth went dry in an instant. I knew this. It was the basics. Stuff you'd talked about on the first day. So why couldn't I think of the answer? Why could I only picture the intense look in your eyes as our foreheads touched, moments after our almost-kiss? "Oh, um, is that the one that stores food and pigment?" I finally said.

Your lips curled up a little at the edges and I smiled back, knowing I wasn't quite right but unable to find the desire to panic. "Perhaps someone should have spent her weekend studying instead of sitting in a salon chair," you said, turning away.

I don't know how a heart can be in two places at once, but in that instant mine was in my throat and my stomach. My cheeks flamed so hot I thought I might burst.

God did I hurt in that moment. I'd spent hours picturing your look when you saw my new hair. Hours imagining your sweet smile, imagining you tugging on a lock of it as you complimented me.

And instead, you slung it back at me like I was some kind of airhead. I couldn't believe you'd done that, Bennett. And I couldn't figure out why. Why you would humiliate me like that, why you had to call me out in such an unfair way. I would never do that to you.

You meant too much.

The review was over then anyway, so why did you make such a point with me? You returned to the front of the class and picked up the stack of tests. Since the desks were in a horseshoe, which I'd loved so much that first day, you either had to walk around or you had to split the stack in half and start it at each end.

That's what you did, and at first I was annoyed—so annoyed, because I wanted you to hand me that test yourself so I could glare at you, feeling more than a little bit juvenile but unable to control my emotions—until I realized I was essentially in the middle of the horseshoe and the extra stack of tests came to me from both sides.

So I held them out and stared at you with a flat gaze, a gaze empty of the emotion I felt for you, steeling myself. Your eyes were soft and maybe a little regretful, but you said nothing as you took the tests and turned away.

And then I sat there, scribbling my name on the top of the page, still angry and hurt that you'd purposely embarrass me in front of the whole class.

The first question was the first thing you'd just reviewed with us, so I felt a smidgen of relief as I filled in the bubble for C, and a little more relief as I read the second question.

But that was all the relief I got. I was only marginally confident in my third answer, and by the fourth, I was lost.

I hadn't studied at all, Bennett, and as I looked at one question after another, I realized that I'd hardly even paid attention to what you'd taught over the past few weeks. And there was nothing I could do. I was smart, but we'd covered a lot of ground, and I'd be lying if I didn't say that I was often distracted by watching you, your lips, your hair, your hands. Sometimes half of what you said didn't even register, because I was too busy daydreaming about you.

I sunk further into despair as I flipped to the second page of questions, glimpsing plenty of terms I knew, terms I remembered from class last week and from high school Biology, but the things I needed to know, the questions you posed, went over my head.

In all my life I'd never taken a test like this, one I couldn't breeze through, and it was miserable. Was this what it was like for students who weren't naturally smart? Who struggled to understand the basics while I soared right on past them, aced the AP courses, and enrolled in college two years before they'd ever have the chance?

I read the questions over and over as the students around me slowly got up, delivered their tests, and left.

I knew, statistically, that C was the best answer, so I used that every time I guessed.

And I guessed a lot.

By the time I looked up, I was startled to realize I was one of two students left, and the other was already handing you her test and slinking out of the room, looking about as happy as I felt.

I pushed my binder into my backpack and zipped it up, emotions swirling in my gut like it was a big blender. I slung my pack over my shoulder and squeezed through the gap between my desk and the next one, my flats quiet on the tiled floors, and then I was standing in front of you.

You sat back in your chair and looked at me, worrying your bottom lip between your teeth as if you were searching for the words.

"Why?" I asked.

You blew out a long breath. "Sorry. I just…got nervous and overreacted."

"Nervous about what? I was the one who was put on the spot like that," I said, holding on to my frayed nerves.

"I don't know. I'm worried people will realize what we're doing, so I was trying to treat you like anyone else…" Your voice trailed off and you looked so genuinely worried, with the space between your brows creased, that I believed you. "And then I went totally overboard."

"That was completely embarrassing," I say.

"I know. Like I said, I'm sorry."

I wanted to stay angry, but it was slipping away. "We're not even doing anything, anyway. We've just talked. And hiked."

"We haven't done anything *yet*," you said, and it wasn't meant to be flirty or seductive, just an honest truth. You stood up and started to walk toward me, and then in a blink you'd stopped, gone back to your seat, and sat down. And I realized you had the same instincts as I did, the same magnetic pull, and then I felt stupid for worrying about the woman in the pencil skirt. You wanted me, not her. "I promise you it won't happen again," you said. "Okay?"

I nodded. "Deal."

You pursed your lips for a long moment, and I stood there waiting, unsure of where we went from here, where we were supposed to take this next. We couldn't kiss, we'd agreed on that, but couldn't we be something else? Something in an area just gray enough that we could ignore the things that pushed us apart and allow ourselves to be pulled together?

"Can we hang out again?"

I'd wanted to hear those words so much that for a second I thought I'd been the one to say them aloud, but it wasn't me, it was you, and you were waiting for an answer.

My lips curled into a smile before I could stop them and I nodded, my streaked hair sliding over my shoulder. I reached up and twisted a strand around my finger as you spoke.

"We don't have to hike or anything. I live on Green Valley Road … maybe you could come over and we could go down to the river?"

It was hard for me not to jump up and down or clap my hands or … *something* to show how excited the idea made me. *Your house.* You wanted to show me the real you, the one outside of the college.

"Yeah, that would be great," I said, letting go of my hair. "When are you thinking?"

"Maybe on Friday afternoon? I just have office hours in the morning and then I'm free … if you are."

I was supposed to help my dad pump up a bajillion new basketballs, something he loathed for some reason, but I would come up with some fake excuse to be with you instead. Dad could get one of his derelict students to help him, and in doing so feel that he was saving the kid. Like he was some Disney movie teacher, saving the day, and the kid goes on to become a doctor instead of a gang member.

Not that we even had gangs in Enumclaw, but that was how my dad saw his job—it was the only way he could find bigger meaning in a career that he thought was beneath him.

"Yeah, that would be great." I beamed at you and you smiled back.

"Good." You pulled out one of your cards and scribbled down your address, then slid it across the desk. "Don't let anyone see that, okay? It's gotta be…"

"A secret," I finished.

"Yeah." Your nose crinkled up. "Wish that didn't sound so…"

"Dirty?" I asked, and then laughed. "I know it's not like that. It would just get…complicated if we didn't keep things quiet. I get it."

"Good. Because earlier, when Zoey was here…"

The pencil skirt woman. "Oh, no," I said. "I mean, I get that you have colleagues or whatever…"

"Right. She's a Chemistry professor. We share the lab and have to work out scheduling conflicts and stuff."

"Uh-huh. I get it."

"Good. I didn't want you to think…"

I didn't supply a fill-in answer that time, because I didn't know what you wanted to say, but I wished you'd finished that sentence. Did you already see how much I'd fallen for you, and you needed me to know that you were saving yourself for me, not dating anyone else? Were you telling me to wait for us, that you wanted things to be exclusive?

You didn't finish the sentence, though, so I'll never know what you meant. Eventually I just said, "No, it's fine, I get it."

"Cool. So, see you tomorrow?"

"Yeah. See you at the lab." I stepped away, feeling suddenly... lighter, more sure of us, of what we were becoming.

"Looking forward to it," you said. And by the tone of your voice, I knew you meant it.

*

ON THURSDAY, JUST a day away from our upcoming time alone together—a day I couldn't stop thinking about—Katie plunked down next to me in class with a sad-puppy face. "So, before we get those tests back, I was thinking I needed to put some pre-emptive good-test karma out there. We need to plan some study sessions because, holy hell, I think I'm going to get a big ol' F."

I sighed as I flipped open my Biology book. "Yeah, me too. I guessed on two-thirds of it. I hadn't even read the last chapter and I totally forgot that we even had a test, so I didn't study."

Katie leaned over like she wanted to share a secret or juicy gossip. She lowered her voice and said, "Yeah, I wondered, because you're way smarter than me and I knew that answer, and he totally called you out. What was that even about?"

My heart tumbled all over itself and my smile turned a little forced. Had she picked up on the fact that you were treating me differently than everyone else? I shrugged like it wasn't a big deal. "I don't know, I guess he was trying to make a point of it or something. Like to scare everyone else into taking it seriously." I flipped another page of my Bio book even though I hadn't read the one I was on. "I mean, I won't make the same mistake again, that's for sure."

She snorted. "Yeah, maybe that was his plan, like make sure people know he'll call you out if you're not pay-ing attention. Kinda harsh, you know? I'm totally paranoid now that I'll forget an assignment and he'll totally embarrass me like he did you."

"He didn't *totally* embarrass me or anything," I said, suddenly defensive even though she was speaking the truth. "I mean, he's right. I didn't read the chapter or anything and I completely flunked that test. There's no way I got more than half of them right."

Before we could talk any further, you stood up and walked to the center of the room, a thick stack of papers in your hands. "All right, guys. I've got your tests back, and I'll be returning them. Remember that the three tests in this course represent forty percent of your grade, and some of you have some real catching up to do."

With that, you glanced down at the first test and walked to the jersey-obsessed guy at the end of the horseshoe, placing the test face down on his desk. I watched as he jokingly made a cross on his chest before flipping over the test, then fist-bumping his seat mate.

"God, I am so screwed . . . " Katie whispered under her breath.

I laughed, but my palms had turned sweaty. My parents would kill me if I got a poor grade in this class. In any class. To them, failing wasn't even something that existed. It was something that happened to other people, people who didn't care about their futures or some crap.

You walked by, sliding Katie's test onto her desk before proceeding to someone three desks down.

"How'd you do?" I asked, resisting the urge to lean over in case Katie didn't want to share.

"Ew. Sixty-one," she said, frowning.

"It's a pass," I say.

"Barely! It's totally going to drag down my grade, and I want to be a nurse! Biology is kind of important." She looked up at me, her pretty eye shadow bringing out the green hues of her hazel eyes. "We really have to study."

"For sure. I can't do another test like that. My grade will shrivel up and die." I was joking around, trying to pretend like I wasn't freaking out.

I'd never gotten a bad grade. Ever. Perfect little Madelyn Hawkins, Ivy-bound since the first grade, didn't fail.

And then there you were, sliding it onto my desk, moving on so quickly it's like you weren't standing there at all. I took in a deep breath and turned it over, and what I saw made me go completely still.

A-.

You gave me an A-.

"You liar!" Katie whispered, smacking my arm. "You totally aced it. Figures. You have this stuff down pat. Well, now I know who gets to lead our study sessions."

You gave me an A-, Bennett.

I know I didn't earn it. You *gave* me that A-. I guessed on so many questions, I couldn't have just gotten lucky. I couldn't have truly earned that A-.

"Yeah, uh, I guess I did better than I thought," I said, tucking the paper quickly into my binder, guilt swimming up my throat and choking me.

Did you change my answers, Bennett? I never wanted to look at that test again, so I didn't check. You either changed them or you simply wrote a false grade at the top of the page, and I didn't think I wanted to know which one it was. You'd said the word "secret" felt dirty, but this felt worse.

My mouth was dry and a sick feeling sat in the pit of my stomach like a bowling ball.

The rest of the day you didn't call me out in class, like on Tuesday, because you didn't call on me at all.

I wanted to say something to you right then, when the class was over, but I knew I couldn't, knew I needed more time to talk to you than the five minutes between class. And besides, I was going to your house on Friday.

Your address on that business card was burning a hole in my pocket.

*

EVEN IN THE FALL, Green Valley Road was lush and beautiful, surrounded on both sides by vibrant green pastures and cedar trees. Cows dotted the fields, and elaborate mansions, set back behind fancy iron gates, popped up each time I rounded a curve. I crossed a bridge that spanned the Green River, the waters surging below me, then followed that winding, two-lane road.

But finally, when my knuckles were nearly white on the steering wheel and my nerves had turned into a painful churning in my stomach, I slowed at an asphalt driveway.

Your address was tacked onto a post where an old pipe gate hung open, so I turned up the drive, following the line of it until a tiny little cottage, partially obscured by big rhododendrons, could be found.

Your little red pickup was parked next to it, so I knew I'd found the right house. Once I put my own car in park, I couldn't help but stare.

I was glad that the house was set off the road like it was, and that there was only one real neighbor, back where the driveway met Green Valley Road. It felt like we'd found a private paradise—somewhere we could be ourselves, just like up at High Rock.

A place we could be just a boy and a girl.

I zipped up my fleece jacket before getting out, warding off the bite of the autumn air. I couldn't help but swing my hips a little as I strode toward your house, hoping my new, snug jeans looked as good as Katie's. I'd curled my newly highlighted hair that day, and it fell around my shoulders in a way that made me feel older, ready for you and for whatever lay beyond your front door.

I stepped up onto the stoop and raised my knuckles to knock, but your door swung open, my hair fluffing in the breeze of it. I froze like that for a second, feeling silly, before dropping my fist. "Oh, hi," I said.

"Hey. Come on in," you said, stepping aside and motioning to the house. You glanced outward, and for one millisecond I was annoyed, because I couldn't help but wonder if you were checking to see if anyone saw me. Then I realized I was being stupid. People really couldn't see us together, and besides, you'd hardly glanced. It was *me* being paranoid, overly sensitive.

"I'll give you the grand tour," you said as I met your eyes. You looked amazing that day, more relaxed. You were barefoot, in jeans and a threadbare, warm-looking sweater. Your hair was product-free, falling into your eyes in a way that made them seem darker, sexier.

"Sounds great," I said.

"Don't get too excited. It's a one-bedroom house, so it's a pretty short tour." You grinned in that crookedly charming way of yours. "In any case, this is the great room," you said, motioning to the space beyond the entry. "Isn't it…great?"

I half-laughed, half-snorted, feeling some of the tension leave my limbs.

A hardwood floor led into the living space, which was modestly furnished with a comfortable-looking brown leather couch and a small flat-screen perched on an antique sideboard. In the corner, Voldemort sprawled across a fluffy dog bed, snoring softly. A big still-life painting—a bowl of oranges—hung on the wall. The painting was a surprising contrast to the eclectic mix of bacheloresque furniture.

"My mom painted that," you said when you noticed me staring.

"Oh, is she an artist?" As soon as the words were out of my mouth, I wanted to reel them back in. *Duh, Maddie.*

You nodded. "Yeah. She has a studio downtown. I mean, it's not really profitable, but she manages to cover the cost of the rental space at least."

I nodded. "And your dad?"

"He's a welder. He probably made half of the fancy iron gates you see on this road."

"Wow, really? That's so cool."

"Yeah, art runs in the family. He only likes to do the gates with something extra to them—silhouettes of horses and cows, or fancy twists in the iron or whatever."

"So you didn't get your teaching gene from them, I guess."

"No. What about you? Think you'll be a teacher of some sort, like your dad?"

I shook my head. "Nah. I mean, I don't really know what I want, I guess. But I don't think I'll teach."

You nodded. "It's either for you or it's not. I love everything about it."

You led me into a kitchen. It was small and a little outdated—with golden-oak cabinets and old laminate countertops in a deep shade of green, oddly—but it looked well used, like maybe you knew your way around a stove. I could picture myself sitting at the kitchen table on the wrap-around bench, watching while you cooked me breakfast or lunch or dinner, or anything, really. I would have settled for broccoli. I'd sit there, transfixed, that yellow swath of light spilling in through the windows, the light so warm and sunny I could stay forever, live my life right in that room beside you.

It burned, that candle in me, growing and flickering into a fire, and in that moment I knew I couldn't go back to where I'd been just weeks earlier, couldn't undo the thoughts I'd had and the things I wanted.

From that moment, it was you, and only you, and no one else mattered. I didn't care about those two stupid years, I didn't care that what we were doing was dangerous in so many ways, I didn't care that I was alone with a man who was almost ten years older than me.

I just didn't care anymore, because the only thing that really and truly mattered to me…was you. But to you, I knew, those two years would still matter, even if not in the law. And somehow, I would have to find a way to tell you.

On December 13th.

"So, the kitchen's not that fancy, but it works and that's the point, right?" you said, grinning. You were back to that boy on the mountain, the one who laughed and smiled and seemed so much closer to me in age.

I never thought of you as a boy when I was sitting in class, yet when we were alone, it was different.

You stepped back out into the great room, leading me down a short hallway. "Bathroom's right here," you said, pointing through an open door.

I peeked my head in and saw a large bathtub/shower with frosted glass, a standard white toilet, and a big oak cabinet—the same age as the kitchen—with an old Formica counter, this time in cream and gold. I didn't really care about that stuff, though, because I was busy surveying the variety of things on the counter: an electric shaver and a razor, shaving cream, a comb, toothbrush … it was all so normal and also so exotic—the idea of you standing there in the morning, barefoot, shaving. I hoped that somehow as you got ready before class you took extra care, hoping to look good for me the same way I did for you, the same way I'd felt while curling my hair that very day.

"It's nice," I said, stepping out of the bathroom.

"Eh, it's outdated like everything else, but it's big enough anyway." You led me down the hall and stepped into the door at the end, where the carpet turned plush, not quite matching the rest of the house, and you flicked on a light. "This is the master. It's the only bedroom, so it's the master by default," you joked.

My mouth felt a little dry as I stepped into your bedroom, as I stood in the place you slept, imagined the covers only partially covering you as you lay there peacefully, alone. As maybe you dreamt of me. I'd be lying if I didn't admit that I thought of us, sometime in the future, together in that bed, under those hunter-green plaid covers.

December 13th would just be a kiss, but maybe someday...

"It's..." I cleared my throat. "It's nice. It suits you."

"Thanks. Although I'm not sure what that says about me. I'm outdated and well-worn?"

I laughed. "No, masculine and... erm... spacious?"

You laughed again and poked me in the side. "You're going to have to work on that."

"Masculine and... nice-smelling?"

"Better."

You flicked the light off and brushed past me in the hall, leading me back to the front door. "I was thinking we could walk over to the river, if you want. There's a trail behind my place. County owns the land. We could walk down there for a bit, until we get too cold, and then come back and have dinner."

"Sounds perfect," I said, and I meant it.

An evening with you.

Alone.

*

THE PATH TO the river was worn smooth, like you'd walked it hundreds of times. The autumn rains had turned the exposed paths slick, but as the sun rose higher behind us, warming me through my light jacket, I couldn't bring myself to care.

When we reached a downed tree, you turned and held your hand out, helping me jump over the log. This time, when I got to the other side, you didn't let go like you had on our hikes. You didn't act like what we were doing was forbidden, had to be a secret.

You smiled at me like a boy smiles at a girl, and I was lost to you in an instant, too far gone to care if it was all supposed to be wrong.

Too far gone to care if you were going to turn your back on me when you found out the truth. On December 13th, I was going to kiss you, and then I was going to tell you.

I don't think that's what people mean when they say kiss and tell.

"Your hair looks cute like that," you said, reaching over with your other hand and tugging at my curls.

"Thanks," I said, blushing a little bit and squeezing your hand, so pleased you'd mentioned it after all. It made that hour cursing the curling iron worth every second. "I like your sweater."

I chided myself then because it sounded dumb, like it was some quid-pro-quo thing. I wish I had complimented you first.

"Thanks... I got it in Paris, actually," you said.

"Oh, I thought it looked familiar. That picture of you and the Eiffel—"

I stopped then, realizing what I'd said and kicking myself.

You raised a brow. "Did I show you that picture?"

"I... uh... no. I saw it on your Facebook," I admitted.

You grinned, revealing a wide row of gorgeous white teeth, saving that single crooked one I'd come to love. "Ahh, you Facebook-stalked me," you said. "I'm so flattered."

"Maybe a little," I said, blushing. "I got curious.'"

Curious. Sudden panic filled my chest. What if he got curious too? I would need to change my Facebook page to private immediately, before he saw I was a student at Enumclaw High School, before he saw all those young-looking faces I'd friended.

Before he discovered the truth.

"And?" he said, his own interest piqued. "Did it satisfy your curiosity?"

I shook my head. "No, it wasn't enough."

"You wanted more," you said, bumping my shoulder. "My my my, whatever will I do with you over the next eight weeks?"

Eight weeks. God that sounded like a long time.

"I have not a clue," I said, batting my eyes innocently. Maybe it was too much—me being young and then trying to *feign* innocence—but I didn't think about it at the time.

The sounds of rushing water, which began as a faint, dull buzzing, intensified to a weak roar, and then we stepped onto the rocky banks of the Green River. I had to put my free hand out slightly as I stepped on the uneven surface, picking my way between the bowling-ball sized rocks. Sandy shores, this was not.

"In the summer this place is packed with tubers, but lucky us, we have it to ourselves," you said, just as you let go of my hand. I wanted to chase your hand, put it back in mine and never let you go, but instead I pushed both of my hands deep into my pockets as the chill had already crept in. I wondered how long we'd last out here, by the almost-icy banks of the river, the air a chilly fifty degrees with a misty breeze coming from the rippling river.

"Do you walk down here a lot?"

You nod. "When I'm not buried in homework to grade, yeah. Sometimes even then. There's something about water that's calming. I think if I weren't a teacher, I would have wanted to join the navy or something. Sail the world."

"It's almost as calming as hiking," I say, thinking of the way you looked at High Rock, so different from the man in the classroom commanding thirty students while dressed in a no-nonsense button-down.

"Exactly. Something about it just … brings a little bit of clarity." You shoved your hands into your jean pockets, and the way they pressed those jeans into your legs made me think crazy thoughts, thoughts I shoved aside. Then you added, "Sometimes just being away from everyone else helps you figure out what you want, you know?"

God I knew what you meant. It was under the roof at home where it was impossible to figure things out. Somehow when I was away from my family—at GRCC, or at the actual Green River with you … somehow the pressure lifted and I could almost glimpse, through the fog of life, who I wanted to be.

"And what kind of clarity are you craving these days?" I asked, watching the way the water rippled around a rock.

You stared at the river, not answering, and then you pulled one hand out of your pockets, leaning down to pick up a stone before tossing it into the river. After the *plunk,* the woods rang with silence. "I'm trying to decide if this is right," you finally said.

"What?" I asked, my mouth going dry.

"Us. This." You glanced back at me for a moment before leaning down and grabbing another small stone, lobbing it into the river in a graceless way like you wanted to see a harsh splash. "I'm trying to ignore what I know every single other person would say, and I'm trying to just think of being with you instead."

The air felt like it'd been sucked out of my lungs, in the same way it's sucked from a room during a house fire. "I thought we decided—"

Your look silenced me. It was somehow fierce and soft at the same time. "We did, and I won't go back on that. I want to see what this could be with us. But——"

"But you've thought about walking away," I said, fear settling over me, like you were going to desert me at any moment. And I was too far gone to handle that. "You've thought about what everyone else would think."

You nodded, but your eyes were trained on the water and all I could see was your thick, dark lashes, as for a moment you closed your eyes and they brushed your cheeks. I wanted to touch them, touch you, but I stayed glued to that spot on the bank, my feet at odd angles on the rocks.

"You're so much younger than me," you said in a matter-of-fact voice, in a way I couldn't refute. "And I don't even know if you're just doing an AA degree, or planning to transfer and move away, or what, and I just keep wondering what the hell I'm doing with a girl fresh out of high school."

I can't explain the relief I felt at the way you'd worded that, because I knew that when I responded I wouldn't have to lie—not so obviously, anyway—because I sort of *was* fresh out of high school. I wasn't going to class there anymore, never would again.

But the "out" of high school didn't totally work, because, really, I was enrolled *in* high school. Formally. Technically. Legally. Just not physically, since I would never go there again unless I needed to for paperwork or something.

Me and you, we were both done with high school.

And yet I also knew, could see... that you were struggling with the idea of dating an eighteen-year-old, a fresh face.

"I don't know yet. About college," I said. "What I want to do, where I want to go, if anywhere at all. I have time."

If you asked my parents, they would explain the plan. They'd had it figured out for me since birth. I had the GET account, the brochures, the flawless transcript. I was going to a four-year college. I would follow in my mom's footsteps. Avoid my dad's *failed* path.

You were the first person I'd admitted the truth to. The first person to whom I said simply, *I don't know.* It was amazing how freeing those three words were, how good it felt to hear them out loud. How much I wanted to admit I had no goddamn idea what I wanted from college, from life.

I wanted you to know how lost I was, but we weren't there yet. I couldn't say those things. And for that moment, *I don't know* was enough.

I blew out a long, weighty sigh, one probably too heavy for our romantic moment. "Don't you ever just get tired of having everything mapped out, predestined, planned? I just want to *live*. Decide which way to turn once I'm sitting at the intersection, you know? Screw the road maps and flip a coin."

You nodded, pursing your lips like you had things you wanted to say, but then your lips just curled a little and you turned to look at me again. "You really are smart."

"Thanks," I said. "Maybe next time you could try not to sound so surprised."

You laughed, and the mood lifted, and then you turned away from the water and walked up to me, and you let your hands settle on my hips as you leveled a gaze at me. "It feels so weird to think I might've met my match in a girl so much younger ... but it also feels so ... "

"Right?" I asked.

You nodded, your lips pressed in a thin line. "Yeah. And that's what scares me. That I feel like I could settle into this ... into you ... without a look back."

"Why is that so scary?"

"Because every sane thought I have is telling me it's not right to date a student. I'm risking everything ... "

"For me," I said, finishing your thought.

You nodded. "Yes. I'm risking everything for you. For the chance to be with you."

"You say that like maybe I'm not worth it."

"There's not a doubt in my mind you're worth it," you whispered, leaning in, pulling my hips up against yours so that our bodies were touching at our stomachs, hips, thighs. It was intimate in a way I'd never experienced, casual in a way I hadn't expected. Like we fit together, were meant to be like that.

I let go of the tension in my shoulders, my arms slackening as I leaned into you, my body fitting against yours, my cheek resting against your shoulder. "I wish this was easier," I whispered. "I wish we'd met some other way, so it wouldn't feel so ... "

"Conflicted?" you offered.

But I wasn't conflicted. I was utterly convinced we belonged together, that we'd always *be* together. And some part of me twinged inside because you'd picked that word, like you had doubts. But I didn't voice this.

"Difficult," I said instead. "I want to be with you everywhere. On campus, at the grocery store. I want to not wonder if someone is watching us right now."

You tried so hard to hide it, but I could feel the slightest tension ripple through you, like you hadn't considered that and the idea that someone was watching us terrified you.

You always did have more at stake. I was stupid, naïve then, and I never quite saw it, but it was always *you* with the risk. Your life, your reputation, your job.

I would always be the sweet, bookish girl who got taken advantage of. That's how the world sees me. Pity, sympathy, sadness ... so many things, but no one who matters is disgusted.

Not like they are with you.

Maybe I needed to be eighteen to get that. Maybe that's where the two years come in. Perhaps they bring the ability to understand what's at stake, to foresee what could happen in a few weeks or months. Because at that moment, on that river bank, I sure didn't possess the ability to look forward and see what was coming.

I only saw you and how much I wanted you. I knew in that moment I had to make you mine, whatever the pain, whatever was in store for us.

I just wish I'd known, that day at the river, that it wasn't my own life, my own pain, at stake.

It was yours.

✳

WE STAYED ON the riverbank for almost two hours, sitting on the rocks until we were both more than a little frozen. It was a different world there, on the shores of the river, where time seemed to stop around us as if that superpower of mine actually worked. But eventually we had to give in to the cold, and we traced our path back to your adorable little house. I leaned into my jacket, wishing I'd worn something a little warmer, rubbing my hands together, willing them to warm, driving away the tingly feeling just as we stepped through your back door and went to the kitchen.

I stayed quiet as I watched you work, pulling things out of the fridge, stepping out back to light the grill, turning and twisting and cooking like you did it every day, were at ease in the kitchen.

My parents thought I was going to the library, then studying with friends. I had never *ever* lied to them like this, and they had absolutely no reason to think I wasn't telling the truth. That's why it was such a piece of cake. Sixteen years of being the model child—screaming inside for some kind of relief and yet marching on like a soldier, doing every little thing expected of me—and in that instant I'd given them the first bald-faced lie, the first one of many that would lead me down to the cliff, the cliff I'd jump right off of in a few short weeks as my lies snowballed.

"It'll be done in a few," you said by the time I'd fully warmed. "There's Snapple and soda in the fridge."

I got up just as you stepped outside to pull the chicken off the grill, stopping to pat Voldemort as I headed toward the fridge. It's funny how different your dog was when he was home, how often he just slept on his bed, occasionally thumping his tail on the ground. So different from the dog who bounded up the trails with us.

When I peered into your fridge, I saw Snapple and soda, but I also saw beer and a six-pack of hard cider and I was *so damned tempted* to grab one, twist it open, and walk out to that patio like there was nothing wrong. I wanted to be old enough to do that so you wouldn't feel so wrong about us.

All I ever wanted was to be free with you, but every time I turned around there were more restrictions, more evidence that I wasn't as old as you were.

So I grabbed a half-lemonade/half-tea Snapple and popped the top, reading the silly little fact under the lid. *Relative to size, the tongue is the strongest muscle in the human body.*

God, I did not need to be thinking of the tongue.

I had to wait to kiss you.

Later, so many people told me that your allure had to do with you being forbidden. Like somehow knowing I wasn't allowed to be with you is what made me want to be with you even more. I don't believe that.

I tossed the lid into the trash and walked outside, to where you were leaning over that grill, the mouth-watering scent of smoked cedar wood and chicken wafting toward me as I plunked down in a plastic chair, no longer worried about the cold, just zipping my jacket up to my chin. "It smells awesome," I said, smiling.

"Thanks. I have to admit I'm a terrible cook, but I can barbecue okay."

"I guess you need a girl for that," I said, surprised at my quick quip. "I can cook a mean lasagna."

Actually, I can cook pretty dang well. I mean, my dad does a decent Mr. Mom act, but I'm better. Since my mom is MIA so often, I'd picked up the slack and somehow found my own gene for cooking. It's actually one of the few things I can connect with my dad about. Those moments in the kitchen when we work together, even wordless, are sometimes the only moments we share.

I held out the platter to you as you pulled off the lid on the grill, setting it on the cracked patio. Everything about this place reminded me of a perfect old pair of sweats, or a chipped, beloved mug. Well used, broken-in, and comfortable, but not flawless. And yet to me, knowing you had your own place, knowing you could support yourself… it was awe-inspiring on its own.

Because as I stood beside you, I realized that I could support myself someday, that I didn't have to have my parents create the way, didn't need them to decide which path I'd take and then pave it in gold for me.

What if I didn't want to go to MIT or Harvard? What if I finished my two-year degree and got an office job and hung around town . . . for you, for me, for us? What if we created our own life and it had nothing to do with them, had nothing to do with my mom and dad's plans for me?

Every second I spent with you was like liberation, was like a way for me to poke holes in their plans, in their requirements, in their expectations. It was only in those moments away from their keen eyes that I felt like I could breathe deeply and figure out who I wanted to be.

I know that if they read this, that means they're going to blame you, act like you're the reason I questioned their college pathway. The thing is, it's not just you. Maybe you pointed me in a new direction, but I chose to open my eyes, I chose to blink and look around.

And as you put that barbecue chicken on the platter, I felt a strange mix of grown-up and relaxed, like maybe the intensity I felt in my life wasn't because of me at all, but them.

And maybe with you I could have something different, could *be someone* different.

A girl who took charge of her life.

I took the platter inside and you followed, after tossing the lid back on the grill and closing the vents to snuff out the remaining charcoal.

I slid the sliding glass door closed behind me, shivering again. I'd planned to dress cuter but that would have required freezing my ass off, so I'd settled somewhere in the middle.

We each picked a piece of chicken and a scoop of macaroni salad and then you led me to the living room. "That window by the table is kind of drafty, so why don't we eat in here," you said, setting your plate on the coffee table. You reached behind us and pulled forward a rainbow-colored blanket. "My mom totally quilted this, so you cannot make fun of it," you said, grinning like you fully expected me to make fun of it.

"Knitted," I said instead.

"Huh?" you asked.

"'Quilted' is like making a patchwork quilt. She *knitted* it."

"Oh." You chuckled. "Okay, so she knitted this psychotic thing. My request still stands."

"Deal."

You settled it over our legs so that our knees touched as we put out plates in our laps. Our forks clinked as we ate.

It should have been awkward, that first time I ate with you, you in that amazing sweater, the one that hugged your shoulders in the way I wanted to. But it wasn't. Even then, it felt good to just be with you. And yes, I wanted so much more, but it was so easy to settle for what I was allowed to have: a quiet meal together, our knees touching, the blanket warming us up to a comfortable temperature.

We didn't talk as we ate, and it didn't bother me. The only sound in the room was the quiet ticking of the wall clock, one that reminded me I couldn't stay with you forever. Not yet.

Somehow we'd reached five o'clock already, and dusk was rapidly approaching.

"Do you have to be home any time soon?" you asked.

"Nah, my parents won't care," I said. Then I cursed myself for mentioning them at all, for thrusting them at you like that.

"You live with them, right?"

I nodded. "Yeah. Just until I'm done with GRCC." I paused. The college only had one small dorm complex, used mainly by international students. Most of the other students still lived at home, or maybe had a small apartment with a few roommates. "I told them I'd be home late."

"Great," you said, like you meant it.

I set my plate down on the coffee table and then let my body settle into the couch, pulling that supposedly ugly blanket up higher, and a surreal feeling settled over me.

There I was, a sixteen-year-old girl, in the home of my twenty-five-year-old Biology professor, watching as he ate dinner. Such a simple, domestic act, something a student was never meant to see.

I glanced out at the windows, to where the fog was settling around the edges. "I can't believe winter is coming soon."

"Winter... and December." You grinned and leaned forward, and for a second I had the oddest idea that you might just curl up close to me. But instead you tucked the blanket over my shoulders, then sat back again so that we weren't quite touching.

"Thanks," I said.

"I'm a Biology professor. If you die of hypothermia, I'm sure the irony would haunt and kill me too," you said.

I smiled, wondering if there was a way to find that superpower and push *stop*, so that you and I could simply sit there on that worn-in old couch, be there for all of eternity, enjoying life without the world to judge us for it.

You must have felt it too? The rightness of it all, when we were together and all those stupid rules just... disappeared?

I really do believe, even as I write this, that sometimes two people are just meant for each other, and that we were two of those people. Two people who made sense, and if only those two years didn't matter, we'd still be those two people today. Bright and happy and comfortable in the warmth of that wood stove, in your simple, unassuming one-bedroom house.

Sometimes what I hate most about all of this is that we never hurt any one. Not a soul, not even me.

Don't they get that? That you never hurt me like they keep assuming? I was *better* because of you. I was someone who mattered, someone who was allowed to have an opinion.

It was my parents who made me feel like a kid. Not you.

Never you.

*

WHEN I WENT downstairs the next morning, I'm pretty sure I floated down the steps, lost in memories of you, in thoughts of how hard it had been to pull myself away from you and drive home. It was dark by then, but my mom and dad hadn't thought a thing of me arriving home so late.

Trust is a funny thing.

"Hey! You're just in time to help me cook," my dad called out as my bare feet hit the tiled floor.

For a jarring second I'd forgotten it was Saturday, forgotten about the tradition of a giant weekend breakfast.

"Oh, uh, awesome," I said, blinking away the memories of you and making my way into the kitchen where Dad was bent over, digging through the produce bin. Without looking up, he said, "You can chop up the peppers. We're doing a scramble."

"Cool," I said, over the din of washing my hands. After I dried them on a paper towel, I went over to the little peninsula, to where the granite shone brightly under the fancy canned lights.

The atmosphere was different than it had been with you just the night before. It wasn't awkward, but it lacked the warmth I'd felt when I'd stood in that small kitchen of yours, watching your able hands prepare dinner.

Here, everything looked so nice and shiny and perfect, the way I was supposed to look.

I grabbed one of my dad's fancy Ginsu knives and set to work slicing the peppers into thin strips, the way he liked it. Dad brushed my arm as he set an onion on the counter top, and then he whirled around again and disappeared into the big pantry at the far end of the kitchen. I glanced back but could only see a shadow beyond the frosted glass door.

He emerged with a whole bag of potatoes, plunking them down on the counter and then turning to grab another cutting board and a big bowl. This was my father at his finest—a constant blur of motion, as if to make up for his stagnant career.

"How's class going?" he asked as he went to the sink to wash the first few potatoes.

"Good. I think I have an A in everything so far," I said, a familiar sensation drifting over me. Grades. A's. All the usual expectations.

Funny, how I felt so different inside and yet he couldn't see it.

"Atta girl," he said, returning to the counter. "How are your professors? Do you like them?"

The knife slipped then, and I yanked my hand back just in time.

"Whoa, watch it," he said, leaning in to peer at my finger. "These knives are no joke."

He'd come too close to the truth.

"Yeah, sorry. Knife slipped." I picked up the red pepper I'd been chopping. "Professors are good. The English one is kind of boring, but Bio is great," I said, going with the truth. You *were* great. You were so much more than great.

"Oh yeah? What are you studying in Bio right now?"

Bennett, I wanted to say. I spent all of my class time studying you. But I didn't think my dad would like that answer.

"We covered cell composition first, and then genetics, and now we're on to evolution. We just had our first test," I said.

"Oh?" He looked up at me, his hands stilling. "How'd you do?"

This was that moment, that look, the one that said, *Don't disappoint me, Maddie. Don't end up like me, wallowing away as a small town PE teacher. I had big plans once. I was going to be somebody. And now look at me.*

"I got an A-," I said, feeling a little bit weird about it. I did get that A-. You *gave* it to me. But Dad didn't need to know that, did he?

"Great job. A little more and you can turn that into an A."

And there it was, that same push-push-push.

"Yeah, maybe," I said. I wanted in that moment to say, "Well guess what! I actually flunked! What do you think about THAT?"

Instead, we let the silence fall, and he finished chopping the potatoes. Then he tossed them in a hot pan with a bit of oil and started stirring, the potatoes hissing from the heat.

"You know what we should do?" he asked abruptly.

"What?" I tossed the chopped onion into the pan, blinking away the tears from the intense onion scent.

"Let's go do the corn maze," he said.

"Uh, what?" Corn maze? What the heck was he talking about?

"The corn maze. You know, at Thomassons'?"

"I haven't gone to that since I was like twelve."

"Yeah, but wasn't it fun?"

I look at my dad, realizing he's serious. His eyes are lit up like a kid who just got a puppy for Christmas. "I mean, yeah, but I was twelve."

"Oh, is Maddie too old to be seen in a corn maze with her dad?"

He grinned at me in a way that made me grin right back without even meaning to. In a way that somehow made me say, "Okay, let's do it," even before my brain recognized that I was excited by the prospect.

*

"Two for the maze, please," my dad said. Behind us, two kids squealed, tickling one another as they impatiently waited in line.

"Here you go," the girl behind the little window said. "Do you want cow questions or sports trivia?"

"Cows!" I said at the same time my dad answered, "Sports."

We looked at each other. "Okay, fine, cows," he said, taking the narrow sheet of paper from her hand and giving it to me.

I don't even know why I chose the cow one, because it isn't like I know anything about cows, but I probably know less about sports, and we *were* on a farm, so it seemed like the thing to do.

My dad followed me across the wide gravel drive and down the little slope leading to the entrance to the maze. Just inside the six-foot corn stalks, a placard greeted us: "*A cow gives how many gallons of milk a day?*" Dad read aloud.

I looked at my paper. "A is four gallons, B is eight. Holy crap, there's no way it's eight," I said, walking left for A.

He followed me and we rounded the corner, and then the maze closed up around me. I stopped abruptly, and Dad knocked into my back before stepping away and giving me some space. He laughed, an easy, carefree laugh I don't hear that often. "Eight gallons did seem like a lot," he said.

"Seriously. Poor cows," I lead him back the way we'd come, now following the arrow for B. We stepped farther down the path, the air growing cooler in the shadows of the cornstalks.

"Okay, next question," I announced. "*Name one of the stomachs of the cow.* It's either 'reticulum' or 'burnum.'"

"Isn't a reticulum like a ladies' purse or something?" my dad asked.

"Uh, no. I think that's a reticule? 'Burnum' doesn't sound like a real word. Let's go with 'reticulum,'" I walked to the left once again, this time slower, in hopes I wouldn't walk straight into a dead-end again. Instead, the path curved around to the left, then snaked to the right, and when I saw the next sign post, I grinned, triumphant.

"Woohoo," I said, feeling silly but not caring. It was strange to get out of the house with Dad. To get out of the pressure cooker and try to guess what the names of a cow's stomach were. But I had to admit … it felt good.

It reminded me of when I was younger, before I hit junior high, before everything was just another item for the college application, before the word "college" even entered my head. Before my parents started asking me where I wanted to go, who I wanted to be.

Back when we used to go to the mall or the park or sledding, a day of outdoors. And yes, maybe Mom was rarely there, but Dad was. He let us just be kids back then, before the expectations kicked in.

Before he started talking about how, in an instant, all of his plans fell through, how we'd have to be more meticulous, plan things better than he did.

We were supposed to be a success story, like Mom. Never a failure, like Dad.

I'd never thought he was a failure.

"See, told you this would be fun. We totally gotta do things like this more often," he said.

"Yeah. I agree. Next time I'm studying cow trivia beforehand." I was laughing.

"You're good at that," he said.

"Good at what?"

"Studying. I wish I'd had your skills when I was your age. You're going to go so far..."

That familiar vise tightened around my heart. "Yeah, I guess."

"One bad tackle and BAM, it was all over for me. Don't make that mistake. What do you think you'll go for? Engineering like Mom, or something else? Hell, you could be a doctor if you want, the way you absorb things like a sponge."

"I don't know," I found myself saying.

"Yeah, we've got about a year to figure it out. Although I guess it would be good to do it sooner. If we study the prerequisites for your degree, we could select your college courses to meet those needs."

"Mhmm," I said, feeling suddenly mute, like my insides had turned to mush and were just rattling around in there.

"I'll look it up this week, figure out some choices."

We finished the rest of the corn maze in silence, and when we emerged at the other end, I didn't feel triumphant.

*

THERE ARE A lot of days that stick out in our relationship, but there's one in particular I know you must remember with a great deal of clarity, and now, looking back, with a measure of sad irony.

We were at your house again, that place I'd been going with increased frequency. The house was so quiet, so secluded, and once I parked my car behind that dilapidated old barn, no one could even know I was there.

We were watching a movie—*Ferris Bueller's Day Off*—partly because I'd never seen it, but mostly because you'd proudly proclaimed it a product of the '80s.

"Not that, you know, I was old enough to see or appreciate it when it was released, but still," you said, sliding the DVD into the player.

"I'll let it slide, since I did take credit for Nirvana and all." I smiled as I slid the drapes closed, shutting out the glare splashing across the television.

"That's right. So we're practically even."

"Except that I've never even heard of this movie, and everyone knows Nirvana," I said.

"Blasphemer!" you said as the DVD menu popped up. "Everyone knows Bueller."

"Okay, old man," I joked.

Your smile slipped the barest bit. "Hey. It's only like what, six years?"

My mouth went dry. Six years. You thought I was nineteen.

It was the first time you'd asked me outright like that, and when confronted with the idea that I had to consciously, outright lie, I couldn't form the words. Lying by omission was so much easier.

A knock on the door behind me made me jump and I whirled to face it. You didn't have a peep hole or windows in the door, so instinctively, I reached for the drapes, intending to peek out.

You were beside me in an instant, grabbing my hand. "Hide," you whispered.

My eyes widened. "What?"

You stepped up to the window and nudged the curtain open with just one finger, then turned to me, your face paling. "It's my mom. Hide."

My jaw dropped, and for a second I wanted to say *no*, or *why*, but then it hit me all at once—who I was, who you were, where we were.

And then I knew I had no other choice.

"Where?" I asked.

"In my room," you said, gently grabbing my elbow and steering me toward it.

I sat down on the bed, but it squeaked slightly. I shifted my weight and it squeaked again.

"Shit. You'll have to go in the closet."

Even as I knew that it made absolute sense, that it was a must, that it was the only way to protect you, I hated it.

I nodded as you opened the closet door while another knock hammered at the front entry.

"Just a second," you hollered.

I stepped into the small walk-in, plunked down on the floor, and leaned back against the folded blankets in the corner.

"I'll try to get her out of here as quickly as possible," you said, your voice low. "Just... don't make any noise, okay?"

I nodded, and as the door clicked shut I couldn't help but be happy there was a light in your closet, and then embarrassed I was sitting in a closet at all.

I heard the door swing open and your voice. "Hey, Mom, what's up?" Your voice was so bright, cheerful... and forced.

I couldn't quite make out her response, but she sounded quiet, down. And like she'd walked inside, because her voice grew louder. Her shoes—heels, I imagined—clicked across the floor, and then a chair screeched on the tile and I knew she was sitting at the kitchen table.

I wondered what she looked like, this artist who made beauty with canvas and paint. I wondered if she was brunette like you, had a crooked tooth and warm blue eyes.

A second chair screeched. You were sitting at the table with her, and where you now were, out of the great room and hall, your voices dimmed.

I sighed and glanced at my watch, then crossed my arms and leaned farther into the blankets stacked on the floor behind me, wondering how long she planned to stay if you were both sitting down now.

I would have to wait her out.

I'm NOT SURE when I fell asleep, only that I was startled awake when the door flung open.

"I am so—" You paused, and the trace of a grin tugged at your lips. "Were you sleeping?"

"Maybe," I said, blinking, more than a little disoriented as I accepted your outstretched hand and you pulled me to my feet. "What took so long?"

You grimaced. "I'm sorry about that. One of her friends in Auburn has been battling cancer and she needed someone to talk to. I couldn't get rid of her without being a total asshole. She looked like she'd been crying."

"Oh."

You glanced back at the closet before flipping the light off. We walked to the couch and sat down at opposite ends. "It didn't feel right," you said.

"What? Getting rid of your mom?"

"No, shoving you into a closet."

I poked you with my toe, grinning. "I would hope not," I said, "or we're going to end up with a really strange relationship."

But your face remained stoic. "No, I'm serious. It was like I was freaking sixteen and living at home or something. I didn't like it. The need to hide you."

My heart clenched. "It's just until December," I said.

But even if that was technically true ...

I was sixteen. You'd only *felt* sixteen, but I was actually there. And I wondered, would you really be willing to introduce me to your mom once you weren't my professor anymore … once you weren't in a "position of power" like the law said?

All this time I'd been looking forward to that day, the day we could be together and not have to hide. But even though the law couldn't judge us, would it matter to you that everyone else still could?

And I would have to tell you, because I didn't want you to do something you'd regret. I'd have to come clean and just *say it* before we took the leap—before you went somewhere you might not want to go.

But it wasn't going to happen on that day.

That day, I wanted you too much to tell you I was sixteen.

I would tell you on December 13th.

I had every intention of doing that, Bennett.

But you know what they say about best-laid plans.

*

Over the next few weeks, you and I spent a lot of time at your house, or down at the river, even as the air grew colder and the leaves blew in the autumn wind. I guess it wasn't that different from hiding in your closet—it was our way of staying away from prying eyes, from questions, from people seeing things they shouldn't see.

We never discussed it, because acknowledging out loud that we were doing something against the rules, well, that would have made it too clear that being together was wrong. So we let it hang there in the background, always present but never in the forefront.

One night, we were lying side by side in your backyard under two thick blankets, staring upward at the stars as the grassy lawn around us turned frosty and crunchy and our breaths came in puffs of white. Even Voldemort, with his thick coat, had lost interest in staying outdoors and retreated to his warm bed inside.

November. We'd been creeping toward winter for weeks, and that night we weren't quite snuggling—that would have taken it too far—but we were so close together that we were touching from shoulder to hip to ankle, and the warmth of your body spilled over to me.

I should have left an hour ago. I knew my parents would be wondering where I'd gone but I couldn't bring myself to say that aloud, and I'd left my phone in the house, on silent, so I had no idea if they'd started calling.

We'd been talking for hours, and there was just no way to peel myself away from you.

I blinked up at the stars, listening to the melodic tone of your voice, remembering how it had sounded on that first day of class, before we were this close, when I was nobody to you.

"She was...beautiful." Your tone was bitter and wistful all at once. You glanced over at me before training your eyes back on the stars. "Not beautiful like you are..." you said, trailing your voice off. And somehow, I wasn't insulted or hurt. Somehow, in just a few short weeks, I'd gained a measure of security with you, known you were putting everyone else on hold for me as you waited for the weeks to wind down. Besides, you were calling her beautiful like it was a fault. "She was like, a china doll, or the stars. Beautiful to see, but untouchable."

I pulled the blanket all the way up to my chin, to ward off the cold that steadily crept into our little eden.

"She was the kind of girl who would walk into a room and people would stare. I knew I didn't have a shot in hell with her, so I didn't approach her like everyone else did. I played pool and ignored her. But then...she challenged me to a match. We played for six hours and never finished the first game because we couldn't stop talking."

I didn't know where you were going with your story, and it was getting harder to hear about her—this beautiful ex-girlfriend of yours.

"What went wrong?" I finally asked, after realizing you'd stopped and the silence had fallen around us. I expected to hear crickets, frogs, birds... but we were too far into fall now, the promise of winter driving them all away.

"We lived together for six months during our senior year of college. We made a lot of plans, about where we'd live, where we'd work. She was studying fashion, and we both knew that would be a hard field to get into outside of New York or LA, so I promised to move so we could be together. And then she got restless. Decided she didn't want everything we'd been planning, and she left me."

"Sorry," I said. Although I wasn't, not really, because if you'd been with her you couldn't have been with me. "How long ago was this?"

"A little over a year." You let out a long breath and a big puff of white appeared above us. "I got home and her closet was empty, and she'd left a note on the counter." You chuckled under your breath, not a laugh with real humor, but bitterness. "Want to know what it said?"

I sensed that you'd tell me either way, so I didn't move, just stared up at the Big Dipper, my eyes following the contours of it.

"*Please cancel my cell phone.*"

"Huh?" I asked. Of all the things to say, that was most important? Not goodbye, or I'll miss you, but cancel the phone?

You chewed on you lip for a moment, lost in a memory, before you answered. "We had a joint plan. She didn't want it anymore."

But... "That's a weird goodbye."

"It meant more than just canceling a plan. It was her way of saying that I'd no longer have a way to contact her. She didn't want me to."

"That's cold."

"Yeah. I thought we'd be something forever. Took me a while to feel whole again."

I nodded, listening to the underlying tones in your voice, listening to the rumble of your chest as you spoke and breathed and lived, wondering how a girl could possibly walk away from a guy like you.

"So, that's my deal. I can be a little gun-shy at times. Sometimes it feels like I'm waiting for the rug to get yanked out from under me." You pursed your lips and stared upward, and as the silence lingered, guilt overwhelmed me. You'd been hurt and there I was, right next to you, my big secret wedged in between us. "So, what about you? Have you ever been in love?" you asked, and in the darkness you found my hand, squeezed it.

I forced away thoughts of the ways that I betrayed you every day, forced myself to believe in our love, in your ability to forgive me and choose me even after you found out how old I really was. The dark of the night and the blanket surrounded us, my hair splayed out on the pillow we shared, our heads tilted toward each other.

So often, Bennett, you kept me at a literal arm's length, careful not to touch me, to get too close. You were restrained. But that night, as you thought of old love, as we looked up at the blanket of stars, you let us lie so close, our palms touching.

And all it did was make me want more, made me shove that secret deeper than ever.

More, More, More. You made me hungry for you with each word, each touch.

"No," I said simply, even though I wanted to lie. Even though I wanted to say I'd had a thousand relationships, prove to you I was old enough, mature enough.

But I didn't think I could fake the details of love, build the kind of story you did, make you believe that there'd really been another guy, a perfect, beautiful guy who was too broken to stay with, who didn't deserve me.

"Yeah, kinda tough when you live at home," you said.

"It won't be that much longer," I said. *Just two more years or so.*

"Nah, don't feel like you need to make an excuse. College is expensive. I mean, I went away to a four-year school, so I lived in dorms until my senior year, but I still stayed with my parents every summer until I graduated."

Yeah, it's expensive. Especially when EHS pays for everything.

"And the first year after I moved out, I'm pretty sure I lived on ramen noodles, and I had three roommates," you said, laughing. I remembered a photo of you at a bar and

I pictured that life, you living with roommates and making your own way. "This place isn't much, but it's a huge upgrade. I'm hoping I can buy it someday. I like the setting. I could always add on to the house."

"It is a nice place," I say. "And everyone has roommates at some point."

"Yeah, but it was three of us... in a two-bedroom apartment."

"Oh," I said, laughing, my breath coming out in puffs of white.

"I mean, we had big bedrooms, but sharing a room when you're that age?"

"Sucks," I said.

"Yeah. Basically sums it up. Life goes on, though, you know? It has a way of getting better with age."

I grinned into the darkness. It was funny how fast the time slipped by when I was with you, hidden under the stars, in a valley where the river wound around and around, where farms dotted the landscape, the monotony broken only by enormous mansions and the occasional, cozy little house. I could build an entire life for myself in that valley.

"Did you always want to be a teacher?" I asked.

Silence ensued, and I wondered if I'd encroached, gone somewhere I shouldn't have.

"Yes," you finally said. "My dad... he's a brilliant welder, but his brain works like my mom's, kind of off the wall, scattered. I'd ask him for help with my homework, and even though he could build these huge custom gates for million-dollar homes, he couldn't conjugate a verb or isolate x in a math equation. And every time I asked, I saw that it drove him crazy. He *wanted* to know those things, but he didn't. And my mom... she's just as talented, but..."

"But neither of them are the book sort of smart," I finished.

"Yeah. Drove me crazy. They're like the Einstein sort of smart. Incredibly intelligent but barely functional. I mean, they'd have money in their bank account and bills smashed into the to-be-paid bin. I always craved more order, structure."

I laughed a little under my breath.

"What?"

"I think my parents are as much the opposite of that as it's possible to be. Meticulous."

"Sounds amazing," you said.

"It's..." I searched for the word, when there were so many options. "A challenge," I finally said.

You squeezed my hand, turning toward me, and when I did the same, our faces were so close our noses were just a breath apart, and when our breaths came out in white misty clouds, it was like they washed over us. Even after everything that has happened with us, sometimes I still think that this moment on your lawn, in the chill autumn night, was our most intimate moment. The moment we saw each other. Not in a physical way, but in a soul-bar-ing, emotional, bonding kind of way, a way that can never really be undone by other relationships, by time or distance. It was the kind of everlasting intimacy that I didn't ever want to experience with someone else.

"You're not like them, are you?" you finally said, your eyes boring into mine, knowing it was a statement not a question.

Moments passed, moments where your words echoed in my ears.

I'd never told a soul that I didn't really want to be like my mom and dad. So many people would pat me on the head and call me a "mini-me" of whatever parent was present. So many teachers compared me to my brother, who they'd had in class just a few years prior.

To them I was a Hawkins. I would be the person they expected me to be, nothing more, nothing less. I would ace the tests, slam-dunk the finals, complete every piece of homework.

And you lay there, and you saw me as someone else.

"No. I don't know what the hell I want," I admitted, my heart lifting from the release of my confession.

"You're not supposed to."

"In my house, it never occurs to anyone that I'd even want to be anything else. It's math or medicine. MIT or Harvard. It's success…or you're not a Hawkins."

"Hard to imagine."

"My dad lives every day thinking he's a failure, and he's made it his mission to ensure that I succeed. And then, on the opposite end, my mom's so damn proud of how she worked her way up in the world—she grew up pretty poor—that now that I've been given all this opportunity, she just assumes I'll seize it like my brother did. They always just assume..."

"Sometimes not being seen at all is worse," you said.

I blinked, just as you did, and I swear our lashes nearly touched. "Yeah. That's how I feel. Like they all know I'm there, but I'm supposed to be this robot, following a course they mapped out a long time ago. Except they haven't even thought to actually ask me how I feel, make sure..."

I trail off. Make sure what? What do I want?

"That you want it? That you haven't changed your mind in the last few years?"

"Yeah, basically. Like they are all so focused on these stupid...*routines*. What if I don't want a freakin' routine? What if I want to live it one day at a time?"

"They wouldn't understand," you said.

A strange warmth tingled through me.

You got it. You totally got it.

"Yeah. They'd freak out and think something was wrong. They'd ask a thousand questions. They'd tell me it was a phase I'd grow out of. Every time I even *think* of saying something, I realize it's fruitless, so I just stand around mute all the time, watching time pass and nothing changing."

"It's no different from me thinking so methodically when my parents are anything but," you said. "When someone thinks differently … they just … do. No way to change it."

"It's maddening," I said, the despair creeping in. "Sometimes I have these weird dreams."

You pulled me against you then, so that we weren't staring into one another's eyes anymore. Instead, you somehow tucked the blanket more closely around us and I was cradled against your body, my lips, my nose, tucked into the curve of your neck, one leg tangled up in yours, my body heat mingling with yours.

Someone could have happened upon us a thousand years later and I would have been happy to be in the same spot.

"It's always the same," I said, the dream creeping in again. "I'm standing at the front of a church." I chewed on my bottom lip so hard it was uncomfortable and then forced myself to stop.

"And?" you prodded, when the silence had stretched out, my breath warm on your neck, my own nose suddenly growing cold from the frosty night.

"I'm standing there, in this horribly clichéd princess ball gown, all in white, and a veil is on top of my head."

"And I'm standing across from you," you said in a total deadpan.

Despite the intensity of the moment, I laughed, poking you. "No. There's nobody there at all. The officiant keeps droning on and on and on … exchanging vows and talking about love … and not *one* person in the pews notices that I'm the only one standing there, that the groom hasn't even shown up."

You didn't respond, but your hand kept stroking the small of my back in an intimate way, a way that made me want to roll over, lie on top of you, straddle you. It took all I had in me not to do exactly that.

"In the middle of the dream, I always rip the veil off and start screaming, but everyone just keeps on with the ceremony, marrying me to this guy who isn't even there."

"Classic dream," you said, a long pause later.

"You think?"

"You want control but you don't think you have it."

"Really?"

"You haven't even picked your groom in the dream. Everyone just expected you to show up in your white dress, and you did what they wanted."

I raked in a deep breath. "That's so … obvious, though." I said.

"Because it's the truth, right?"

"Or maybe it's about love or whatever. It's a wedding dream."

"Who's in it?"

"Huh?"

"Do you know any of the people in the dream?"

My teeth slid together, clenching as I pictured it. "My dad. And my mom. And weirdly... my brother is the officiant."

"Why would your brother be in it?"

"I don't know. He's always been good at one-upping me. I guess if it's my wedding, he'd want to be the one doing all the talking, somehow being in the limelight. Plus, I don't know. He's always so in control of everything."

You chuckled then, and it was like everything I'd said was stupid, shortsighted. Yet you didn't make me feel dumb for everything I'd said.

"You know..." You turned into me, like I'd done to you, so that your arms wrapped around me and we were fully entangled, our breaths entwined in clouds of frosty white. "There comes a time where you decide to be yourself."

"Easy for you to say," I mumbled into your skin.

"It's not. Easy, that is." Your voice was soft and forgiving.

"Really?" I asked, surprised.

"It's not easy for anyone to break away from what they're used to," you said. "But that's where you find yourself."

"Spoken like a man who knows it all," I said, partly to push the topic away from myself, and partly because I wanted so much to learn more about you.

"Oh God, I wouldn't say that." You chuckled in a way that made your breath hot on my skin, such a stark contrast to the frosty night, the night that had grown so much darker while I'd been with you.

I should have left hours earlier. I should have been home right then, in my bed, or at the dinner table … or whatever was appropriate at that moment. I didn't even know what time it was, and I couldn't bring myself to ask you, to extract myself from your limbs, to walk across that yard and check my cell phone.

"You'll come around," you finally said. "I wasn't totally sure what I wanted when I entered college either."

But I knew you'd been eighteen, maybe nineteen then.

"It just takes some distance. Some perspective."

"The ability to live outside of a ginormous shadow," I said, but now I was murmuring, feeling sleepy as I spoke into your skin, nestling closer to you, feeling the soft, worn T-shirt, the all-too-rigid fabric of your jeans against my khakis.

"Exactly. It takes distance. No one works on a sculpture without stepping back and taking a look. Life is like that."

"You're way too smart for me," I said under my breath, my eyes closed, welcoming the heat of your skin and the way it somehow permeated me, found its way under my clothes and pulled me against you.

"We really should get inside before we freeze to death," you said after a long beat of silence.

"Mhmmm," I said. I knew we couldn't stay out there all night. We'd both be shaking within the hour, and there was no way in hell I could get away with just ... disappearing for the night.

But when I was against you, my legs against yours, your arm around me, your hand sliding up and down the soft skin at the small of my back, your lips resting against the skin at the base of my neck—knowing, restraining from kissing me—oh God, it was impossible to think of December 13th, impossible to remember why we weren't making out, why I couldn't swing my weight over six inches, why I couldn't lie against you, why I couldn't part my lips and slip my head to the side to kiss you.

I wanted a lot of things that night, but I would have settled for a kiss.

*

A DAY LATER, after another two hours of Biology in which I listened to that perfect voice of yours, I floated through the front door and up the stairs, rounding the corner to head down the hall, and that's when I slammed into my brother.

"Oh!" I said, stumbling back as he grabbed my coat to keep me from falling backward down the steps. "Sorry, I was spacing out."

I started to step past him, then stopped, taking in his sweats and old T-shirt. "Why are you dressed like that? Didn't you go to your fancy internship today?" I narrowed my eyes. "Wait—isn't it in Seattle? How are you home already?"

"Um, no…" he said, but the words trailed off, and it was more like he was asking me than telling me.

I pulled off my jacket because up there, next to the vaulted ceiling and overlooking the first floor, the heat from our wood stove was overwhelming. "What aren't you telling me?"

"What makes you think I'm hiding something?" he asked, stepping back and then retreating to his room. I followed him, standing at his doorway while he flopped down on his bed.

"Do you not like it or something?" I asked, my eyes sweeping over his room, taking in the stack of Xbox games that had tipped over and slid all over his floor, the dirty pile of laundry and socks strewn about, and the half-eaten plate of nachos. We'd had nachos two nights before. Ugh.

"Oh, I don't know," he said, staring at the ceiling.

"Well, if you don't know, shouldn't you, like, be there right now figuring out what you think of it? Sometimes it's just boring because of orientations and trainings and—"

"There was never an internship," he interrupted, sitting up on his bed. "I made it up so I could avoid telling Mom and Dad that I was failing Harvard."

My jaw dropped and I stared at him—my perfect brother with perfect grades, now surrounded by old dinners and dirty clothes and... "How is that possible?"

"I'm not smart like you," he said, his voice both resigned and bitter.

I frowned. "You graduated high school with almost a perfect 4.0 every semester."

"Yeah, almost perfect, not *actually* perfect like you, and my classes weren't even AP. And do you have any idea how hard I had to work to get what I did? To prove I could? It's not easy for me like it is for you. It's like I'm a square peg trying to fit into a round hole, every second of every day. And it worked in high school, but Harvard is different. I bet I wouldn't even have gotten in if Mom wasn't an alum. I mean, when you're there, you can't fake your way through. You either have it or you don't. And I don't."

"So, what, you're just not going back?"

He shrugged, staring up at me with eyes so lost that I suddenly felt like I was the older sister, not four years his junior. "You've been there for two years already. Surely you've got what it takes," I added.

He lay back on the bed again, his legs dangling over the edge. Long moments floated by, but neither of us spoke. I didn't know what to say, and he didn't *want* to say anything.

A car rolled by outside, the muffler banging and sputtering.

"Why do you do it?" I asked.

"Do what?"

"Keep trying to be someone you're not." I leaned against the door frame, waiting.

"Because it's who I *want* to be." He interlaced his fingers on his chest, his elbows resting on the bed beside him. "You know, successful, like Mom. I like math and engineering. It's fascinating. I just can't keep up with it."

His words rang in my ears, and the horrible irony of everything crept up around me. And then I laughed, a little chuckle at first, and then long and loud, leaning over to clutch my sides. He lifted his head and gave me an odd look, then rolled his eyes and laid his head back down.

I slid down the wall, kicking a plastic 7-Eleven cup out of my way, and sat there until I regained my breath.

"So, let me get this straight. You want to be smart like me, so that you can become Mom."

"Yeah. I never could have done Running Start like you are. You're so far ahead of where I was."

"And I don't even want it," I said, shocked by my own honesty.

He picked up his head again and stared, bewilderment laced into his features. "What? Why not?"

"I hate it. Remember that part in *Titanic* where Kate Winslet says she could see her whole life ahead of her, one boring party after another? It's like that. Except swap party with test, with reports, designs, drawings. Math, long commutes..."

"She designs freaking *airplanes*. There's nothing cooler than that."

"There has to be," I said with conviction.

"Then what do you want?"

"Not a clue. I don't get why everyone thinks a sixteen-year-old is supposed to have it all figured out. All I know is ... something else. Something beyond this. Something that's not been mapped out for a thousand years. A trail that wasn't blazed by Mom, or..."

"By me," he said.

I nodded. "Stupid, right? I don't even know which way to blaze. I just don't want to follow you."

"That's not stupid," he said, surprising me.

"It feels like it. A couple weeks ago, Dad wanted me to figure out what my major will be so that I can map out my coursework for upcoming years. *Now*."

"And you said?"

"Nothing."

"Jeez, Madd, we don't live in the 1950s. You have choices. Tell him what you want."

"I don't know what I want," I said, my frustration boiling. "That's the whole point. It's just like when I told Mom I wanted to quit ballet, and she told me if it wasn't ballet it had to be something else. Except I had no other ideas. So I did ballet for three more years before I decided violin sounded more fun."

"And when you quit violin ... "

"She made me take up soccer even though I'm not at all athletic. You know her. The default setting has to be *something*, never *nothing*. So if I can't decide what to do, why not just coast along with the status quo?"

"The status quo is high school. You're in college."

I rested the back of my head against the drywall, then stared at a broken Dorito on the carpet. "I know, but it's all part of the master plan. Graduate with an associate's degree, hit up the Ivy League for two years, have a bachelor's by twenty and a master's by twenty-two. Score an awesome job. Make Mom proud. It's like watching paint dry. And not even an original painting, but a paint-by-number painting."

"You're really complaining that you have every option in the world at your feet and you want none of them," he said, his voice suddenly changing.

I looked up, surprised, and saw he was sitting up again, no longer looking relaxed or distressed, just looking...annoyed.

"Well, I mean, it's not really like that. I'm not trying to complain..."

"You always were the chosen one," he said, standing up so fast his bed creaked.

And then he was out the door and bounding down the stairs before I could figure out what had just happened, what I said to tick him off.

I SPENT FOUR hours working on your birthday cake, and it was perfect.

I stood there and iced it with homemade buttercream frosting. I hadn't known how to make it a mere six hours earlier, but I did then, thanks to Google and a few recipe sites.

It scared me, celebrating your twenty-sixth birthday. Before then, we'd had nine years between us.

Nine.

But that day—in just one day—it became ten. Ten years separated us. It might as well have been a hundred, for all the fear streaking through me that afternoon as I poured and mixed and baked.

As I turned the oven off, Mom walked in.

Mom.

Walked in.

Panic clenched me like a vise grip as she click-clacked her way across the tiles, and my mind searched around, desperate for an explanation. Thank God I'd already decided not to add the decorations until I got to your house—the final touches that would spell out *Happy Birthday, Bennett.*

So it didn't say that when Mom walked in, smiling in that vaguely fake way of hers, that way that says she's going through the actions more than feeling the emotions.

"Hey," she said as she rounded the corner, hanging up her purse, hardly looking at me. "How's it going?"

"Good," I said, rinsing out the bowl, the one that was still covered in batter.

"Something smells good," she said, fluffing her hair up as if to reclaim the helmet-hair look she'd left the house with. She looked tired, in that moment. Her hair reminded me of a turtle's shell, meant to protect her, meant to put on a strong, resilient front.

But it didn't work and she just looked tired.

It was weird how in that moment, as I stared, I realized that my mom's perfection wasn't so glossy, so shiny, so perfect. Maybe she thought she knew what she wanted, but maybe sometimes it changed.

Maybe she didn't have every single piece of her life figured out.

As she smiled at me with smudged lipstick I couldn't help but wonder if maybe we were all faking it. If maybe me, my brother, you, her—if we were all just doing our best, figuring it out as we went along.

"Cake sounds awesome," she finally said as she started to leave the room.

And then I wished I'd kept that last bit of batter, made some cupcakes for my family.

"It's for Katie," I said, lying. Again. As always. Somehow it had become such a norm. I lied to them, I lied to you ... maybe sometimes I lied to myself.

"Oh." She paused, glancing back at me, her overly mascaraed eyes looking ... tired. Overworked.

"You okay?" I asked, surprising not just me, but her. She hesitated at the base of the stairs, caught off-guard that I'd asked.

"Yeah. Tired, you know? We're working on a deadline. But it's good..." Her voice trailed off and then the moment lasted longer. "You? Classes and everything are good?"

I nodded, feeling strangely... relieved. That she'd asked. That she'd taken that one single moment. "I'm doing all right."

"Great. Because... I know I'm busy, *really* busy, but..."

I wanted to reply, wanted to fill in the blank... but I didn't offer. I just stared.

"Well, you know," she finished, lamely.

"Mhmmm," I said, turning to the oven.

"Okay, well, I'll be down in a bit," she said, disappearing up the stairs.

"Yep," I whispered to her non-existent face.

Of course. I knew where to find her. I always did.

Maybe someday she'd find me.

★

THE EARLY DAYS of December—as we grew closer and closer to that fateful night—were the hardest. Hardest for so many reasons. I wanted to touch you, be close to you, feel you.

The river was too cold, so we spent a lot of time pent up in your house. That day, you were at one end of the table, grading assignments from one of your other classes. You'd insisted that you couldn't grade anything from our 9:00 class in front of me—like somehow this would make me not your student, keep those two pieces of our lives from crashing together in a blaze of catastrophic explosion.

I wanted to memorize the way you looked in that instant, your hair really falling into your eyes now—it had grown longer during the quarter—the afternoon light glinting the faintest bit on your five o'clock shadow, your lips curled around an eraser as you chewed on your red pencil.

Quietly, I tapped on my phone, picking it up just enough to snap a picture of you.

The picture that would prove to be our unraveling.

I set my phone down and, when it thunked on the oak table, you glanced up, studying me for a second before setting your pencil down.

"Next week," you said.

"Huh?" I asked. My feet were propped up on the third chair, the one between us. It was the only way we could sit without getting distracted. You'd cooked for me, some kind of chicken and rice dish that was still baking in the oven, and the smells permeated the kitchen.

You said once you were a terrible cook, but you were being modest. I would have happily eaten dinner with you every night. I wanted to someday cook beside you, handing forks back and forth, digging for spices, maybe even going grocery shopping and dog-earing our favorite recipes from that old cookbook you had.

"Finals will be over," you said, intensity gleaming in your eyes as you looked at me. "Friday."

"Oh," I said, my heartbeat spiking.

Next week.

December 13th. The day we'd finally kiss.

The day I'd have to tell you the truth.

Is it possible to anticipate a day with constant, overwhelming eagerness... and dread it in almost equal measure? It was like the moment at the top of a roller coaster, as your heart slams into your throat and you're overjoyed at the idea of swooping down, yet terrified too.

"I was thinking..." You set your pen down, leaned back in your chair. "Some friends of mine have a cabin up by Crystal Mountain. I was hoping we could use it. Grab some food and hot cocoa or whatever, and then drive up there in the evening and stoke up the fire and stay the night."

My mouth went dry and a herd of excited butterflies swarmed my stomach, swooping and spinning in a way that made me both giddy and nauseous.

A kiss.

All I'd ever expected was a kiss.

All those weeks, I'd been so busy thinking of that moment on High Rock when you'd promised me a kiss...

And I hadn't really thought through what would happen after that. I'd been too busy freaking out about telling you I was sixteen, so I hadn't let myself dream of things beyond that day.

That was the only time I felt like a naïve little girl around you, Bennett. That moment I realized that you wanted us to spend a night together. A whole night in a cabin alone, with no one to bother us.

Older girls, eighteen-year-old girls, they usually had experience. They knew what they wanted, and they were comfortable with that. And even though I'd told you I hadn't ever been in love, part of me thought that you must figure I had *some* experience. I didn't know if I could tell you I had none—that I'd never even made out with a guy.

I didn't think you'd judge me, but I didn't want it to change the way you looked at me. I didn't want to give you that moment where you could step back, cock your head to the side, and really *look* at me, finally seeing the cracks in my façade.

I didn't want your mind to finally go to that place, the place that asks, *how old are you ... really?*

"I mean, I don't know if your parents … " Your voice trailed off. You didn't want to bring them up anymore than I wanted you to, but it had to be said, because you knew I lived with them and not in the tiny dorm complex on campus.

"They're not my keepers," I said, waving your concerns away as if it was that simple. "And it sounds amazing. I'd love to. On one condition," I added.

"What's that?"

"You build me a snowman."

And that's how I agreed to go up to the mountains with you, Bennett.

If only I'd known how much we both would change by the time we came back down.

FINALS WEEK STRETCHED on, and on, and on. The worst part of it all was that our final took place on Wednesday, so that was the only day I saw you, and we didn't even get to speak. I'm confident I passed the test—without your help—but the quarter wasn't over until Friday. So for the forty-eight hours leading up to our getaway, I didn't see you, didn't talk to you.

But I thought of you.

I shopped for the perfect outfit, and I bought scented lotion, and I asked myself over and over and over what the hell I was doing. And despite the fact that I couldn't exactly answer that question, I knew there was no way I was backing out. I had to see you again, I had to kiss you, and I had to tell you the truth.

A simple three-step process, when I really looked at it:

See you.

Kiss you.

Tell you.

But when the evening finally arrived and I sat in your truck, my nerves a tangled mess, it was hard not to picture every horrible outcome that could happen once you knew the truth about me.

I didn't want you to be disgusted by me. Disappointed. I didn't want you to be so angry you'd leave me at the cabin and just drive away.

A thousand scenarios played in my head like a horrible blooper reel, so clear that I could see myself losing you and falling apart. As we pulled up to the cabin, my nerves multiplied and jumped in my stomach, but I couldn't take my eyes off it—the place I'd kiss and tell, the place you'd learn the truth.

The cabin was everything I'd imagined. Made of logs but small and unassuming, like it actually worked with the forest rather than being some fancy-shmancy resort like the ones closer to Crystal, the ones that rented for four hundred dollars a night.

You pulled your truck up near the door, easing to a stop like you weren't sure if your truck might slide on the snow and ice. I grinned nervously at you as you put it in park.

December 13th. All that time counting it down, obsessing over it, and then there I was with you and nothing stood between us. The thoughts, the fears, the hope— it all swirled in my head, my stomach, my heart.

You opened your door and, before I had time to open mine, you were there, grabbing the handle. As it swung away, it sucked everything in the cab out with it, sucked out my fears and trepidation, because there you were, standing there, staring into my eyes, ready for me—and it felt so right, I forced myself to let go of the fear and hang onto the hope.

Even though we'd spent twelve weeks getting to know each other, somehow that night felt like it was our first night. Like we'd just met, like you were courting me in some kind of old-fashioned way. I couldn't stop the butterflies from flooding my stomach like a swarm of locusts, but now it was in a good way, in a way that made it impossible not to smile right back at you.

Before I could move, you leaned into the cab, like you were just going to unbuckle my seat belt. But as your body crossed mine you froze, tipping your chin toward me until our noses were inches apart, until it became impossible to breathe.

"I've been waiting more than two months for this," you said, leaning in until the distance between us was less than an inch. I closed my eyes, waiting for it, waiting for your lips to crash into mine. The clicking noise brought me back to reality as you released my seat belt and finally pulled away from me, giving me the air I needed for my screaming lungs. "But we should get inside first..."

My eyes flew open and a blush rose to my cheeks as I realized you'd been helping me out of the truck, not leaning in to kiss me. I nodded, almost unable to speak, and climbed down. The snow was thicker than I'd expected, and as my feet sunk into it I tripped, knocking into you. You grabbed my elbows, pulling me upright, my boot narrowly escaping being sucked right off my foot.

"Thanks," I said, my voice sounding breathless as I leaned into you. You had on your thick leather jacket, the one you occasionally had hanging up in the classroom, and calf-high snow boots. My own Uggs were pathetic with their traction, and I felt as if my legs would go different ways at any second.

"I'll grab our stuff. We need to get a fire going or we'll freeze tonight," you said, your voice husky. I could think of another way we'd warm up, some other way you had to have been thinking about in that very instant as you whispered against my neck. But you didn't voice those less than gentlemanly ideas, so I saved them for the visions that were dancing through my mind.

Visions that overwhelmed me with nerves and excitement until it was like I could barely breathe without feeling shaky.

You held onto my elbow, keeping me from falling as you led me toward the big oak door of the little cabin, its roof so packed with snow I had no idea what color or type it might be. All around us, cedars and fir trees soared, so tall and thick I couldn't see any other homes, or even the highway we'd driven in on. The trees must have been forty or fifty years old, so buried in snow they sagged, as if at any moment they'd release the weight holding them down and then sigh in relief.

But above all, it was the silence I noticed. No birds calling, no rain pattering the roof, no cars driving by on Highway 410, likely because just a few miles down the road the gates were closed, the pass shut down for the winter as it was now completely impassable.

"It's beautiful here," I said as I stepped up alongside you at the front door.

"Yeah, I think so too," you said. "I'd live here if I could. It's so quiet … serene … I can't imagine paradise is really some place on the beach, you know? It seems like it could be here."

And strangely, I had to agree. Because to me, paradise was wherever I could be with you in the way I wanted to be. And if that was a quiet cabin captured in snow, then it was paradise indeed.

You shoved an old brass key into the lock, twisted, and then the door creaked open, revealing nothing more than a dark, shadowy interior. A few flicks of your wrist and the old fluorescent lighting flickered on, humming in a low buzz.

The cabin wasn't large, and it was rustic, but it was exactly what I'd pictured. An authentic but newish log-framed couch was shoved against one wall, directly across from an old TV. Beyond that, the living space became a kitchen, the carpet ending and the linoleum beginning. The kitchen was small, just right for a getaway, okay for packing sandwiches or macaroni salad or hotdogs, but too small for day-to-day living. It had a tiny island and little L-shaped cabinets on two walls, with a stove shoved in along one side.

The ceilings were a tad low but the place was decorated exactly like it should have been, with adorable little signs for the ski-slopes—obviously not authentic to Crystal, just signs like you'd see at Applebee's or someone's lake cabin, made to look old with crackled paint edges or partly worn white-wash.

The painting hanging over the couch had a girl in a gigantic ski suit, her poles sort of flung upward like she was about to crash, her vibrant, fake blond, feathered hair splayed out around her as her ear warmers somehow retained her body heat.

Across the room, over the TV, an aerial shot of Mt. Rainier printed on a canvas—not expensive, but a nice touch—beckoned.

"This is awesome," I said, approaching the photo and staring at it. "I wish I was bad-ass enough to ski this. It must be intense."

Intense. Like the night would be, between us.

"I know, right? My buddy has snowboarded part of it."

"Wow. Intense," I said, then wanted to smack myself for repeating "intense" for a second time in a span of thirty seconds. Did you figure out, then, just how nervous I was? As I rambled about nothing at all, trying to fill the space in a desperate attempt to act casual?

I was completely over-compensating.

"Yeah. We should go skiing in a few weeks, when the slopes open. Not Mt. Rainier or anything, but Crystal. I'm okay at it. I can handle the blue runs and some of the diamond stuff, like Rex. We'd have fun."

My heart soared at that. The idea that we would plan things beyond that night. I'd spent so long thinking of December 13th. Nine weeks prior, at High Rock, you'd put your forehead against mine, and all you'd said was *I can't*, and all I could think was *but I want to*. And now we were there and I knew, by the way you acted ... the tension almost palpable as you unlocked doors and flicked on lights and brought our things in ...

And there you were, planning for what we'd do together *after*. What we'd do tomorrow, next week, this winter.

You pictured us together. For so much longer than one night.

You never wanted me as a fling, you wanted me as your girlfriend. As your one and only, in the same desperate way I wanted you.

I plunked down on the edge of the couch as you started a fire, realizing in that moment just how freezing the cabin really was. I glanced around but didn't see a thermostat.

"It doesn't take long to warm it up, and by then I'm sure we'll be okay," you said, your grin a little lopsided, like you didn't want to be too bold, too assuming.

There was a nervousness to you, too. Because that night wasn't some flippant move, something you took for granted.

You'd thought and anticipated and planned. Not in a weird way, in a romantic way. You cared about me and you wanted it to be everything I wanted it to be. Maybe when they read this, it's going to read all wrong. Like one of those horrible *To Catch a Predator* specials, where a guy schemes his way to a girl. But it wasn't that way.

It was never that way. Not with you and me.

"I can manage," I said, as if I hung out in snow-clad, mountain-top cabins every day.

By the time you were done building the fire I'd gotten out all of our snacks, spreading them out on the table like a Vegas buffet comprised of chips and dip and snack mix and carrots and crackers and a million disconnected things, but things we both loved.

Then we sat down and ate and talked.

And talked.

And talked.

We talked all night, until we fell asleep right there in the light of the fire, and we never even kissed.

Love you forever,

Madelyn

Dear Bennett,

I had to start a second letter, one not meant for them.

That last part was a lie, and not even a good one. You'll probably laugh when you read it. But see, when I wrote everything up to that last page, it was for a reason.

I was going to send it to the police station as a way to clear your name. As a way to show that you'd been honorable, that *you* were the victim here, that you hadn't conditioned me, hadn't groomed me to fall for you. Those are words they used when they talked to me. Ugly words that sounded like total garbage. Words that angered me. Disgusted me.

They didn't understand what we were.

But it turned out that writing that fake ending may not matter at all, so now I might as well write out the rest of it. Because I can't bear to write so many pages of truth and end it all with a lie.

I didn't unpack some bogus picnic while you were building the fire. I simply sat and watched.

Your efficient hands built the fire in no time, creating a little kindling teepee and setting it all aflame, not so different from the warmth that was growing inside of me. As that fire took off, that candle burning within me burst, grew into an inferno. I didn't sink into the couch, like I once had at your house, because every nerve ending in my body was standing on end. Every second, we were creeping toward a moment of no return.

Every day I spent with you, every word we said, every innocent touch, we'd crept toward this night, the night you would kiss me.

But the thing you should know, the thing everyone should know, is that in that moment your back was to me—as you stoked the fire, leaning in and blowing and poking at it, shepherding it from a tiny flame into a roaring fire—I had time.

I had time to tell you the truth.

I had time to confess.

I had time to look at you and tell you that no, I couldn't do this, that I wasn't who you thought I was, that taking one more step down this road could lead to disaster for both of us.

It was me, Bennett, that let this all happen. I held all the cards. I looked at them, knew what they all meant, and I surged ahead anyway, dealing you a hand from which you could never recover.

I wanted what I knew would come next. I was desperate to kiss you, finally, and it meant more to me than anything I'd experienced before it. I wanted to know what it would feel like to be with you without a thousand things between us.

I'd once promised myself that you would know the truth that night. December 13th, the day we'd been waiting for. Before anything serious happened, I'd confess it all. But as I sat there, picturing just how I'd say it, the words simply didn't form. They ran through my head, the million ways I could tell you:

I'm sixteen, I could blurt out.

I'm actually still in high school, I would say.

Do you know what Running Start is? I'd ask.

But as that fire warmed the room with its orange glow, I said none of those things. I simply watched as you walked away, tossing our backpacks onto that little island countertop, your back to me, your shoulders so square in that jacket. And then, as if you'd heard my thoughts, you turned around and crossed the living room in front of me, hanging your jacket on a peg I hadn't seen before near the front door.

I wasn't wearing a coat, and I shivered a little, and you smiled down at me, like you'd seen it all.

And then a moment later you were next to me on the couch and your warmth wrapped around me like a warm blanket, not intrusive or overwhelming, just… perfect and comforting.

"I can't tell you how much I've thought about this…" you whispered, your breath hot on my ear, intense in a way I'd not expected, and I leaned into you, melting.

Your lips brushed my earlobe, lightly at first, and then you teased it between your teeth, nibbling in a way that set me on fire, made me crackle and burn like the fire growing in the hearth, the one that was shockingly warm already ... or maybe that was me, warming from the inside out.

"God I want you," you said, and with those four words, I was yours. Any real thoughts of telling you the truth melted somewhere in the back of my mind.

I leaned back against the couch, pulling you into me, and you responded in kind, falling against me until we were halfway horizontal, and then you seemed to have a better idea, and you halfway stood, pulling me with you until we were both on our feet, swaying, me against your body, more unsteady than ever.

"Follow me," you said, your voice huskier than I'd ever heard it.

I would have followed that voice anywhere. The voice that made my stomach squirm and my skin turn hot.

Your grip on my hand that night wasn't the same as it had been before. It was hot and tight and it pulled me in a way that held urgency, and I couldn't resist it.

In an instant, we'd crossed the main room and I was standing in a bedroom, a place where the only light came from the reflection of the white snow outside. It cast the room in a romantic glow, soft, serene, pale. It couldn't have been staged that way, but it was like a movie set, perfect for the night.

I stood there awkwardly for a moment, my heartbeat out of control, until I felt your hands on mine again, then on my hips, and then your lips on mine, hungry, desperate.

And then we were kissing in the way I'd craved weeks ago, on the porch at High Rock as we'd looked down on the world and you denied me what I wanted most.

That night you gave it to me. Finally, you gave it to me.

You were all over me in that second, hungry, touching, feeling, exploring, needing, and I met you in every way. That candle that had flickered and bent and grown inside me turned into a five-alarm fire, and I was aflame.

You kissed everything, cheeks and chin and lips and neck and collarbone, and I couldn't stop the hungry exploration of your skin as I did the same, until a mattress hit the back of my knees and I toppled onto my back and you followed, until you were lying on me, just as hungry as ever, kissing, touching, caressing, your hands sliding under my shirt.

In that moment, there was nothing else. Nothing outside that room, that cabin, the *world*, that would have torn me away from you.

Not even the truth.

My skin grew hot and when you pulled away a little, I followed, unwilling to let your touch go so easily. Once you were upright, your fingers found the lower edges of my shirt, and then it was slipping over my head, my hair tangling and then falling around my shoulders, the sensation silky and sexy all at once in a way I'd never experienced.

I stayed sitting up as you kissed me, your tongue darting in and out of my mouth, your hunger seeming to match the burn inside. An atomic bomb could have gone off and I would not have noticed.

I was lost to you.

I reached down and grabbed at your shirt, eager to feel your skin on my fingertips, and you pulled it over your head, then slid your hands over my hips, up my back, until they found the place my bra clasped. In a breath, in an instant, the elastic let go.

I should have felt something, then. Shyness. Embarrassment. Fear.

All I felt was hunger and certainty. I wanted this.

You should know that, even now as I look back, I don't regret a moment of that night, not for me, but I do regret it for *you*. I would never rewind it except maybe to save you from what happened afterward.

But for me, for everything that fell apart in *my* life, I wouldn't change it for that, because it was a night I will never forget, never let go of.

You lay me back again, and the rough quilt, the one with elk and moose all over it, the one so suited for this cabin but so unexpected for my first time, felt vaguely rough against my skin, but I couldn't stop touching you, feeling you, wanting you, so it barely registered.

There were zippers and kisses and whispers, heat against the cold—I remember that with amazing clarity, how cold it was in that room, so cold I could swear our breath fogged into the night, but in the dark, I couldn't be sure.

And then there was me and you and the moment, the moment we finally jumped.

Me, you, and the night.

We jumped.

HOURS LATER, I untangled my limbs from yours as the dawn crept into the room. Not through the curtains, but from the main room, the place we'd never returned to after.

The air in the cabin wasn't as cold as it had been when we arrived, though, so I figured you must have gotten up in the night, stoked the fire. It cast a warm orange hue around the living room, the one with all that log furniture and kitschy cabin memorabilia.

I stood in the middle of it all for a long moment, the blanket from the foot of the bed wrapped around my shoulders, looking at it, taking it all in, memorizing it.

It's weird how I had this feeling, like I needed to memorize that dawn moment, like I wouldn't experience it again, like I'd need to catalog it and hold on real tight, make sure I never let go of the memory.

I must have known, right? That it would go all wrong.

I was sixteen, but I wasn't stupid.

All that time, all those weeks, and there I stood, in the afterglow of us finally, truly being together, and I felt oddly … lost.

Because I'd focused all my time, all my thoughts, on that moment. And now that the moment was over, it hit me with shocking clarity. There, standing in the middle of that cabin, I realized I'd been willing to do anything for twelve weeks, been willing to lie and create a whole new me for you …

But I hadn't told you the truth yet, and I couldn't hold on to my lie for another two *years*.

Years, Bennett. That one word hit me like a hammer to the head as I stood there alone in the glow of the fire, listening to it crackle and pop, warming the room while I felt suddenly so cold, down to my toes. I reached over, found your discarded Seahawks hoodie and pushed my arms inside. I pulled it over my head, breathing in the scent of you as my emotions warred.

I wanted you so desperately, I loved you so thoroughly, and in that moment, alone in the dawn light, I realized I would probably lose you.

Even then, I never thought it would actually happen the way it did—so abruptly, so cruelly—but some part of me realized that I could never keep you, that you'd never belong to me in the way I so desperately wanted to belong to you. No more than a child can bring home a puppy and keep it a secret, because at some point the hidden lie grows and barks and demands attention. And that was to be my relationship with you.

You would want more…and my parents would figure it out…and I was only sixteen.

I closed my eyes and took in a few deep breaths, calming down as your scent wrapped its way around me. It wasn't just the hoodie. You were on me, on the blanket, and it calmed me, reminded me that I was still with you, at least for now.

So I decided to ignore the future, ignore the growing secret, the one that would be too much so soon, but the one I could hold for now, the one that could be just me and you and nothing else.

I had no way of knowing the days, weeks, maybe months we could have together before it got complicated…

No way of knowing that everything would fall apart in the next *hour*.

I walked to the bathroom and slipped inside, flicking the light on only once the door was almost closed. But it seemed stuck, like I'd have to give it a shove for it to fully click, and I didn't want to wake you, so I allowed a crack of light that probably filtered into the bedroom.

Under the harsh light of three incandescent, yellowy bulbs, I stared at myself, trying to see me the way you did. Like a pretty college girl, someone you could be attracted to. A girl who didn't look like the one my mom and dad and brother saw.

I did look older, different, sexier in some way. Worthy of your attention, wrapped up in your hoodie, my hair wild around my shoulders.

And then I began to hope that somehow, someway, this wouldn't be a one-time thing. Somehow I'd hold it together. And I knew you didn't see it as a one-time thing—you'd waited twelve weeks so that we could be together.

Not one night, not one time, but forever.

And as I stared at myself in the mirror, I had trouble seeing myself as the girl who would sit on her bedroom floor and pretend to work on homework just so her dad would be happy.

I used the bathroom and washed my hands and then arranged my hair around my shoulders in a sexy way, just in case you'd woken up while I was in there.

I wanted you to see me and want me again. I didn't know how long I had with you, but I had that morning, and somehow I'd make it stretch on and on. I'd figure out a way.

I walked out of the bathroom, flipping the light off as I stepped back into the bedroom. I glanced up at the bed, surprised to see that you were awake, pulling a blanket off the floor into your lap. In the process, my backpack tumbled over, spilling the contents of the front pocket.

I was just in time to see you reach for that pumpkin-orange sheet of paper, the one that fluttered at your feet. And in that moment, my entire world shattered, and nothing else I'd been thinking, not the fears or the hopes, the reality or the dreams...

None of it mattered, because you'd just found the truth.

I FROZE, HALFWAY between the door and the bed, halfway between what we'd become and where I knew we were about to go. Every ounce of blood drained from my body as you unfolded the sheet, your eyes darting across the words on that stupid, *stupid* piece of paper.

I wanted to lunge at you, yank it out of your hands and come up with some way to explain it in a way that would make you understand.

You jerked slightly as you finished skimming, and then you went still, your breathing turning labored as your fingers tightened, gripping the paper so hard your knuckles turned white. You didn't look up at me at first, but you knew I was standing there, waiting.

Dreading, fearing, breaking.

"Why?" Was all you said, your face gray and ashen, your control unraveling.

"I—" And on that one tiny word, my voice cracked, just like the fissure splintering through my heart. You still didn't look at me, just stared right at that page, unblinking.

"Why. Do. You. Have. This?"

And then you stood and were across the room in an instant, standing so close I was forced to crane my neck to look up at you. And when I saw the fear and the rage swirling in your eyes, it became impossible to breathe, let alone speak, and in that moment I knew the thoughts racing through your head, knew that every thing you knew about me was rearranging, creating an entirely new image

You tipped your chin down, just the tiniest bit, until our noses were nearly touching, and you met my gaze with such fire I stepped back.

"*Why*," you growled.

You knew why. You had to have known. There's only one reason why a girl would have a high school newsletter, the one I'd grabbed from the mailbox at home two days ago and shoved into my backpack without giving it a second thought. Every professor at GRCC knew that Running Start existed, that a small percentage of the overall student base might be high school students. They'd probably mentioned it to you in passing, sandwiched between budgets and construction and mandatory office hours, and you'd never thought of it again.

As you stared down at me, those thousand puzzle pieces clicked back together and you finally saw the picture you'd somehow missed all along. You *knew*, but you wanted desperately for me to give you some other reason.

And in that moment, *I* wanted desperately to have another reason, to lie, to patch up the giant crack that gaped between our feet, separating us. That beautiful vision I'd had earlier—of us together, somehow surviving the next two years—it fell into the ocean that now separated us.

"Because I'm still in high school," I whispered, closing my eyes, bracing myself. For what, I'm not sure. I didn't expect you to hit me or shove me, but I had to brace for the impact of the truth.

"How old are you?" The words came out so low and guttural, so drawn out, that it must have been painful for you to speak them out loud.

I took a deep breath as the dam holding my lie back finally broke, and the impending wave washed us away. "Sixteen," I whispered, still not opening my eyes, still not facing you.

Not facing the truth of what I'd done.

The door crashed open and slammed against the wall so loudly I jumped, my eyes popping open because I hadn't heard you crossing the room, and yet once I looked at the place you'd been, all I saw was dead air, emptiness.

And before I could move, I heard you. Heard you retching into the snow bank outside, heave after heave, such an ugly sound compared to the things you'd whispered last night, compared to the heavy breaths and the soft, sweet sounds that had torn from your throat. I slumped to the floor and curled over, closed my eyes against the sting of the tears already spilling over my cheeks, listening to what my lie had done to you.

You went silent a few moments later, but by then it was hard for me to breathe. Yet I couldn't bear the idea of you seeing me that way so I scrambled toward the bathroom, desperate to pull myself together, like that would somehow fix the ugliness of what I'd created. I turned on the sink, splashed cold water over my face, then blew my nose and stared at my reflection in the mirror for only a moment before turning away.

I couldn't look at myself.

I stepped out of the bathroom and there you stood, near the front door, one hand on the door jamb as if it was all that was holding you upright. You stared me down and it took everything I had to meet your eyes. You didn't speak, not even a single word. *Not one.* The moments swirled around us, the clock ticking but the moment stuck.

"It's not illegal," I said, desperation leaking into every word. "I looked it up. Sixteen is the age of consent in Washingt—"

"Do you think I fucking care?" you said.

You never cussed.

"I slept with a fucking *sixteen-year-old*!"

The words rang out around us, falling like anvils, and my throat was so dry I couldn't speak for long moments.

"I'm sorry," I finally said, my voice so sad and empty.

"Don't."

"But I'm—"

"Don't." The words were spoken with such absolute vehemence it broke me all over again, spun my world and tore it apart. Because in that instant, I knew. Knew you couldn't forgive me, knew I'd done something so horrible you couldn't even find the words.

I'd lost you, just like I'd feared.

I swallowed and nodded, making no effort now to stop the tears. Your eyes swept over me for a long, silent moment and I think you must have been asking yourself, *How could I not have noticed she looked so young? How could I have not ASKED her?*

Maybe that's not what you were thinking at all. Maybe you were trying to keep yourself from throttling me. Maybe you felt as broken as I did. Maybe you were watching our future—that thing we'd talked about so often—slip through your fingers over the issue of two measly years.

Why did those two years have to matter so much? In the eyes of the law they didn't matter at all, not once you weren't my teacher anymore. But I knew they mattered to you, mattered to everyone around us.

Was I really going to change that much in two years, become a different person, someone worthy of being loved by you?

You crossed the living room and grabbed your bag, then shoved your clothes in and zipped it shut. You glanced at me once more, and your look said it all. I scurried over to my own bag, ignoring the pain in my chest, the dark gaping nothingness, and picked up my stuff, yanking my jeans on. I wasn't even wearing a bra or T-shirt underneath the hoodie, and it suddenly didn't feel so soft against my bare skin.

I followed you into the snow—the sparkling white that had been so beautiful the night before now looked deathly, cold and empty.

I slid into the passenger seat and you fired up the truck and the silence in the cab was so heavy I felt like I was choking on it. You hit the gas so hard the truck almost fishtailed in the snow and gravel. You barely saved it, and then we were on the pavement, hitting the highway.

It was early, around six, and the few cars on the road were going the opposite way, toward Crystal Mountain, with snowboards and skis strapped to the roof. That morning, whenever there were no other cars in sight, it was almost like we were the only two people left on earth. I kept wishing that was how it really was, so that those two years wouldn't matter, so we could just be what we wanted to be without any repercussions.

I pressed my lips together to try to keep the bottom one from trembling, but it was impossible to breathe through my nose so I had to stop.

"*Why?*" you asked again. You didn't look at me, just stared straight out through the windshield, your face all hard lines and shadows in the early morning light. "Why would you do this to me?"

How could I make you understand? How could you possibly see why I'd done it when all you could see was the number sixteen?

"I wanted to be with you," I finally said.

"In what world could we be together? You're fucking sixteen!" You slammed your fist into the wheel, making the horn chirp as your shoulders heaved. You never cussed, and you were already up to three or four that day. "You're a fucking kid!"

The anger turned abruptly into something else—pity and disgust and fear, and you slumped, barely keeping your eyes on the road. "Oh God, you're just a kid."

And I knew in that moment you were thinking of what we'd done last night. And the sound of the repulsion in your voice broke me in a way nothing else had.

"Please don't," I whispered, bringing my feet up onto the seat and resting my forehead against my knees.

"Don't what?" you snapped.

"Don't make it sound like what we did is so ... revolting."

"It is! Don't you understand that? What we did ... that never would have happened if I'd known!"

You were back to anger again, which was easier to handle.

I looked up at you, the tears streaming down my cheeks unhindered, my throat raw and my eyes burning as everything shattered all around me and I had no one to blame but myself. "But I'm in love with you."

You laughed, an ugly bark of laughter that was like stomping on my already broken heart. "You don't even know what love is."

It was such an ugly thing to say. I knew what I felt, what I still feel as I write this, days after we left the cabin. I was in love with you, and I'm still in love with you. Maybe you don't think I'm old enough to feel true love, but I can promise you I am. Maybe when you're done reading this, you'll finally understand.

"I had to lie," I said again.

"No," you say, a single word. The only word that mattered. There was a finality to it.

A decision.

I turned away and watched all those soaring fir trees stream by the window in a big haze of green and brown, blurring until they didn't exist anymore.

We were never going to have a happily ever after.

*

You still didn't know where I lived, and I had to give you directions through town. I bet you were kicking yourself then, realizing you should have asked, realizing you should have paid more attention to the clues. Then again, it was a community college, so most of the freshman still did live with their parents.

Besides, it wasn't like I could have introduced you. You were my professor, and so eager to hide our relationship.

And that's how I was able to lie for so long. Because we'd agreed to the secret... even if you hadn't really known what you were agreeing to.

"The yellow one," I said, pointing to an old colonial on the right-hand side of the road. You slowed, then stopped at the curb. You didn't look at me, at the house, at anything but the road, and yet I doubt you even saw the road either. You were staring straight ahead, your eyes sort of glazed, your grip on the steering wheel unwavering, like it was the only thing holding you together.

I glanced up at the house, and it took only a half a second for suspicion to rise through my limbs. I blinked and scanned the windows.

Lights.

"Benn—" My voice cut off and I blinked again, twisting around to glance behind your truck.

Across the street sat a dark blue Dodge Charger, the windows tinted.

Fear snaked through me, white hot as I glanced back at the house again.

Too many lights. It was half past six, and my parents never got up before eight on a Saturday. It was the one day my mom let herself be human instead of a robot.

I yanked my backpack off the floor.

"You have to go," I said, my voice trembling. "Now." I shoved the door open so fast I tumbled out, narrowly saving myself from falling face-first onto the ground. "I'll tell them nothing happened. That we talked for hours and that's it. Got it? *Nothing happened,*" I said. The desperation in my voice must have registered, because you looked at me with an entirely different expression: confusion.

"*Go,*" I said, my voice rising, giving away my panic.

Behind me, the front door of my house squeaked, followed by the slapping sound of the screen door as it snapped shut.

I closed my eyes and swallowed as dread hollowed me out, made me feel remorse unlike anything I'd ever felt.

Will ever feel.

I turned around to see my parents standing side by side on the front porch, my mom clutching a crumpled tissue, looking shockingly disheveled, her once-perfect bun loose and hanging down around her face as she held her housecoat tightly around her.

I stood in front of the door to your truck as if to block you from view, as if there was a way to get you out of this unscathed.

But then someone stepped out from behind them, and it was all over.

It was a cop.

*

EVERYTHING ELSE HAPPENED in alternating slow-motion and high-speed. My parents rushing across the lawn in an instant, the subsequent too-tight hug suffocating me for hours. The sound of your truck's engine cutting off in a split-second, but the thudding noise of the cop's shoes across the lawn echoing on forever.

My mom's arm was draped around me as she led me toward the house—but I wrenched away, turned back to see you.

You didn't do the same. The officer walked you over to his car and you leaned against the trunk, your shoulders hunched, your face pale. My mom just kept pulling me toward the house, murmuring something about statements, but I couldn't seem to process it all.

It took a few hours of talking to the police officer, my parents, and then the cop again before I figured out how it had all gone down, what they'd been doing while we were together, and that it was all my fault.

All my fault.

See, Bennett, I'd been so focused, so excited about our getaway, I'd left something important at home: my cell phone.

Everything unraveled over a stupid cell phone.

My mom had seen it on my bed when she went to put away my laundry that night. She thought I'd want it—she knew how attached I was to that thing—and so she decided she'd earn mother of the freakin' year if she brought it to me at Katie's house. I'd given her Katie's address weeks prior, when I'd convinced her to drop off a notebook that was necessary for our study session.

She'd had to go pick up some take-out or something, anyway. So she dropped by Katie's house.

And I wasn't there.

But then, you know that, because I was with *you*. Katie tried to cover for me, but she actually made it worse. She said I was *supposed* to come over that night but hadn't arrived yet. Mom told her I'd left three hours ago, that I should have arrived. And so she freaked out, imagining me abducted or dead in a ditch or in a car accident off a ravine or something.

It never occurred to her that I'd simply lied, that it was a little cover-up. Because to her I was still that Very Perfect Daughter, with the perfect grades and the perfect clothes and the perfect "yes please" and "thank you."

She went home and she figured out my cell phone password, since I'd been dumb enough to leave it on the factory default: 1, 2, 3, 4. And when the screen came to life, it was all over.

That picture I'd taken of you grading papers, your small kitchen behind you … it was my homescreen.

The second she saw that, she called the cops, claiming an older man must have been romancing me. And in that instant, they labeled you. As something ugly, something so far from who you really are.

With those words, it became serious, and the cops put everything they had into finding me. See, Mom gave them permission to search my room, and they turned it upside down looking for more clues. They found that silly note you wrote me one day when I'd been particularly quiet during Bio, the one you'd signed *Bennett* and slipped to me as I left class.

And they found my schoolwork, and your name stood out. That name no one else has, that name I thought was so pretty, so perfect for you.

I was right about sixteen being the age of consent. They told my mom several times that I was old enough to make my own choices, that it wasn't illegal if I was seeing an older man.

But when they discovered you were my professor, everything changed.

As it turns out, it doesn't matter if you'd stopped being my teacher forty-eight hours before we were truly together. Because they say you used your influence to manipulate me, put me in a compromised position.

While we were still gone, they sent people to your house, Bennett. As I write this, I don't know if you've been back there yet, but if it looks like my room did, I'm sorry.

And so as dawn approached, they kept a unit at my house in case we came back. And when you dropped me off we walked right into their trap, their ugly accusations. My mom led me into the house even though I was unravel-ing; she closed the drapes and wouldn't tell me what they were going to do to you. She refused to give me any answers because all she wanted to do was pose the questions.

Oddly, my mom burst into tears that day, something I couldn't remember ever seeing before. She hugged me, because all the time we'd been gone, she'd been convinced that some ugly predator had lured me away. They didn't know it was me fishing, me reeling you in, me lying.

My dad stalked back and forth in our kitchen like a tiger in a too-small cage, his fists clenching and unclenching, his neck and cheeks too red.

I told them we didn't have sex, Bennett. I told them you didn't know I was sixteen and we'd just been hanging out. You can see that in the way I wrote my first letter, by the way I left it hanging like nothing had happened.

See, that letter was going to be my way of explaining everything, to you and to them all at once, redeeming you, making them believe nothing occurred between us, that it was all innocent. But I guess it didn't end up being that in the end. That's why I can be honest now.

They used ugly words, like "violated" and "taken advantage of" and "statutory." Mom tried to push me to go to the hospital with the cops, to get tested or something, and it was Dad who sided with me. I think he so desperately wanted me to be telling the truth that he latched onto the idea that it hadn't happened at all.

I don't know if they could have forced me to go. Maybe somehow. Maybe it's a law or something. But after a few hours of asking me to, over and over and over, they acquiesced and let me make the decision.

I hope you know what my decision was.

Two DAYS LATER, I lay on my bed, in the corner, a place I'd hardly left since you'd dropped me off.

"So you don't *actually* have it all together," came a voice near my bedroom door. "I was kinda thinking you were some kind of cyborg."

I lifted my head to meet my brother's gaze as he stepped into my room and flopped down on the pink bean-bag chair in the corner, stretching his lean legs out in front of him. Sometime since he'd come back home he'd started dressing like he used to, in baggy cargo pants and T-shirts, less Ivy League and more... mallrat.

"I wish. If I was a robot I wouldn't feel anything right now," I said, staring up at the ceiling. I was desperate to feel nothing. Nothing would be so much better than this tortured mixture of guilt and heartbreak, a sort of weight that pressed me into the mattress so that it seemed like too much work to move an inch. I could spend all of eternity just staring at the popcorn ceiling. Truth be told, I kind of missed the stars and posters that used to stare back at me, those things I'd ripped down in my cleaning frenzy weeks ago.

"Plus, if cyborgs don't have feelings, they wouldn't have done the shit I did in the first place," I added.

"*And* you're cussing. Who are you and what did you do with my sister?"

"She was bored, so I got rid of her." Bored. What a stupid reason to do what I did.

It wasn't just boredom, anyway. It was so much more than that. It was loneliness and fear and despair. But how could I explain all of that to my brother, the guy who'd followed a plan like he was a laser-guided missile? Even if he'd failed, he knew what he wanted.

"Bor*ing*," he said.

"Sh—I'm boring?" I asked, twisting a strand of hair around my finger. The highlights I'd done to impress you were fading by then. A literal symbol of our relationship deteriorating.

God I missed you.

"Past tense, obviously. I think sleeping with your professor makes you something other than boring." He cleared his throat. "It's really disgusting, actually."

I picked up a throw pillow and tossed it at him, but I didn't bother seeing if it hit its mark because my eyes were still trained on the ceiling. He grunted, so I took it as a positive hit.

"I mean, dude, the guy is like six years older than *me*. What were you thinking?"

Judgment. No one would understand why I'd fallen for you because they all saw your age. Funny, how I'd focused so much on *my* age and they were all focused on yours.

"I believe the consensus is that I *wasn't* thinking," I said. "I've been told that quite clearly."

"Somehow I doubt that's your own assessment. Come on, tell me. What's going on with you?"

I sat up, surprised that he was being so ... caring. So calm, patient. My parents, the cops ... they'd all clearly formed their opinions of you, of us, before we'd even arrived back at my house. No one needed ... no one *wanted* to ask me why we'd done what we did.

Why I did what I did.

Hell, they didn't even ask me *what* I did, not in a way that begged a real answer. They accused, they stated, they demanded. They'd filled in all the necessary blanks on their own, vilified you as they saw fit.

And for two days, all I'd done was sit in my room and alternate between staring at this same ugly spot on the ceiling, twisted up in guilt, and writing to you, page after page, until my hand hurt so badly I had to stop. And still our story wasn't done yet.

"I don't know," I finally answered, sitting up just enough that I could lean back against the wall. Just above me, a corkboard hung, mostly empty after my cleaning binge. "It just ... happened. I let him think I was eighteen."

"That's still really young," my brother pointed out, but not in an accusatory way. He was the good cop to my parents' bad cop, acting as if he wouldn't judge me for things. Acting as if we could be friends like we once were. I wasn't sure if it was the truth or an act. If he genuinely cared, or if Mom had sent him up here.

"I know, and he struggled enough when he thought I was eighteen. We never would have—" I cut myself off and blushed. "I mean, we didn't actually *do* anything—"

"I call bullshit on that," he said. "I wasn't born yester-day. Or fifty years ago like Mom and Dad, when maybe people were a little more naïve and innocent like life is like on *Leave It to Beaver* or *I Love Lucy* or whatever lame-ass show is set in the decade they were teenagers."

I narrowed my eyes. "No, really, we didn't—"

"Mom and Dad *almost* believe that, but it's because they *want* to believe that. You stayed the night with him, Madd. If it walks like a duck…"

I rolled my eyes but stopped trying to lie, instead opt-ing for silence. I couldn't tell him, not without risking your world, if anything was left of it.

"Are you okay though, really? This all seems kinda…drastic."

I nodded. "Yeah. I mean, I don't know what's going to happen to him and I'm freaking out about it. Mom and Dad won't tell me anything. He's probably sitting in jail or something."

"He's not," my brother said, and my heart squeezed. You weren't in jail, like I'd been imagining for the past two days? And if that was the case, why did the guilt still seep from me?

"How do you know?" I asked.

"I *may* have eavesdropped," he said, not sounding the least bit guilty.

"On who?" My heart raced. I'd been desperate for information but too afraid to ask, not that anyone was around to tell me anything anyway. I was on house arrest, period, and they'd talk to me again when they weren't so upset (Mom) and angry (Dad).

"Mom and the cop who came by this morning. You were still sleeping. They sat on the front porch just below my bedroom window."

"And?" Geez, he needed to just spit it out already!

"They never formally arrested him. They brought him in for questioning. The cop told Mom that these cases are really tricky and *you* would have to want to press charges for it to become anything. Technically, it was illegal, but he said they don't try to prosecute stuff like this unless they think they've got an iron-clad case, because they don't like to drag victims—"

"I'm not a victim," I said abruptly. I wasn't. Victim was an ugly word. I was in love. You'd made me feel things for the first time, and that didn't make me a victim.

He sighed, annoyed. "They don't like to drag *girls like you* through the process unless they're confident they can win."

Girls like me? What was I, if something other than a girl who'd fallen in love with a guy who wasn't allowed to fall in love back?

"So Mom and Dad can't be the one to press charges? You're sure about that?" I asked, still scared. "They seemed like they wanted to nail him to the wall."

"No, I guess it doesn't really work that way. Like I said, it's gotta be you to push the issue, and since you both claim nothing happened and you refused to go to the hospital, they have no evidence. He won't have any charges brought against him."

The relief was strong and swift, and my brother must have seen it on my face. "Don't celebrate yet. He's not really out of the woods."

I stared, waiting for the other shoe to drop.

He played with the strings on his hoodie. "I may have also eavesdropped on a phone call..."

"And?"

"Mom called GRCC. I think he's going to be in very big trouble."

I knocked my head back into the wall a few times in frustration, wishing someone would come save me from the never-ending waves of guilt. Of course. We may have waited all that time to kiss, but it was irrelevant if they knew we'd been ... *fraternizing* while he was my professor.

"I see," I said, feeling more hollow than ever.

"Pretty sure it's going to cost him his job," my brother said. "I mean, I didn't hear the other side of the conversation, but Mom was pretty convincing and I don't see why they'd want to defend him."

My heart wrenched at that. You loved your job. You were so good at it. I'd watched you grade papers, I'd stared while you were lost in lectures, seen the way you guided the not-so-gifted students during labs. Your job was your passion, your identity, your life, all wrapped into one.

It was me who'd cost you your job. *Me.* I was just as guilty as a robber who stole in during the night and took your riches, except what I'd taken was priceless.

"Oh," I finally said, because there was nothing else to say, nothing to defend.

"You have to have seen that one coming," my brother said. "A guy like that can't be—"

"He's not *like that.*"

"He fooled around with a sixteen-year-old student." My brother shuddered then, almost theatrically, and it got under my skin. No one would understand who you were to me, the kind of guy you'd been. They simply wanted to see you as a monster.

"I told you, he thought I was eighteen. And it wasn't fooling around. We spent the whole time just talking. Non-stop talking. He listened."

"What do you need him for, anyway? He's ten years older than you, so I kind of doubt he identifies with teen-age-girl problems. And besides, I'm your brother. I know you better. I'll listen," he offered. "I've got a whole lot of free time on my hands these days. And considering I told Mom and Dad about failing out of Harvard about two hours before Hurricane Maddie hit, I probably owe you one for making me look like the golden child for once."

I wanted to laugh, but I didn't quite have it in me. "So that's the silver lining, huh? You fail the Ivies and the parents don't care because I fucked up worse?"

"Two cusswords in one day! I think I like the new Maddie."

I did laugh then, just a short, sad laugh, one that hurt because a few days ago I'd been laughing so much, with you by my side, feeling like I wasn't just on top of the mountain but the world.

I leaned forward and rubbed my face with my hands, weary. "Why am I so selfish?"

"Everyone is selfish, Maddie. It's part of being human."

"Why do you sound like the Chinese guy from *Karate Kid*?" I asked, looking up.

He mimed the wax-on, wax-off thing, then shrugged. "I've spent the last few weeks with too much time on my hands."

"So what are *you* going to do now?"

"I don't know. I'm thinking UW. It's gotta be easier to crack than Harvard. I only have a couple more years to go, but they'll be the hardest classes. Maybe a lighter load each semester or something. It will take longer, but if I have less classes, I'll have more time to study for each of them, and I could always hire a tutor, since the tuition is so much cheaper..."

"So you're still going for it? The whole engineering thing?"

He nodded. "I told you. I love it. Just because I suck at it doesn't mean I don't love it."

"Life is weird," I said, sinking back onto the mattress and staring upward, again, my eyes finding that familiar pattern.

"You said it," my brother said, and I could tell by the creaking noise of the bean-bag chair that he had stood up.

"Anyway, when you're finally ready to talk, I have a feeling I'm going to be just a thin wall away... for a long time."

"Oh joy," I said, listening as he retreated, listening as his door clicked open and shut, listening as his television crackled to life.

A single tear escaped before I squeezed my eyes shut.

My brother wanted engineering, but in that moment, all I wanted was you.

God I missed you.

*

It was another day before I officially found out what had happened to you.

After questioning you that day, they let you go and you went home. I don't know exactly what they said to you, but my imagination went wild, filling in all the blanks thanks to those CSIs and NCIS shows.

I imagined they made thinly veiled threats, said stuff like *don't leave town* and *we have our eye on you*. They'd make you feel like a bad guy, like someone everyone should be worried about, like you'd go after their daughters too if they weren't careful.

I found out you were free because the cops stopped by to talk to me again, giving me one last chance to press charges. They asked leading questions, pulling me in circles, confusing me, trying to make me accuse you. I guess small-town cops don't have much to do but talk.

Finally I told them I was done, that I just wanted to move on. I told them I'd never see you again anyway, that the class was over, and I think that helped.

But once they said they'd close the case and left, the sound of the door slamming was shockingly loud, echoing in my heart.

The case was done. Just like our relationship.

And now I don't know what else to write.

I STARTED WRITING to you a month ago, back when I thought you were in jail. I thought maybe my letter would help get you released, because they'd see this was all my fault, and they'd see that fake ending where we didn't have sex. I'd write it all down, and then they'd know the way it all happened.

But I didn't end up sending it, of course, and every day it sits in my room, this giant reminder of us. I have every last page, up to the fake-out cabin evening, in the bottom drawer of my desk. The rest is hidden under my mattress, because I'm freaked out Mom is going to raid my room like she did while we were at to the cabin, even though things have died down now and she hasn't done anything like that since she realized I was okay.

They still eyeball me sometimes, study me, like they're trying to figure out how they hadn't seen it all coming. Like maybe there's going to be some evidence on my skin, or deep in my eyes, something to give them the answer they'll never really understand.

But in the end they're all so happy to just move on, believe I'm okay. So here I am, still stuck on you as the world spins around me, forgetting about us.

I don't know what I'm supposed to do with these hundreds of pages, because I guess I don't need them to keep you out of legal trouble.

But somehow I still want you to have them, want you to see why I did what I did. I don't know what you've been thinking these last few weeks while we've been apart. If you hate me, or miss me like I miss you. If you remember the conversations we had, the moments we spent together when we let down our walls, shared our secrets.

If you do read this, I hope you don't hate me for some of the things I included. It was because I thought being honest and sharing a little bit would help them believe we didn't go all the way, and the almost-kiss at High Rock ... I wasn't sure if that was okay but I thought that, if anything, it showed you had restraint, it showed you were relying on what I'd told you and making appropriate decisions based on that, and that you would have done the same if I'd told you I was sixteen.

So, now that I have nothing else to write, I've decided ...

I'm going to try to give you all these pages.

Tonight.

I've tried to figure out another way to do it—a way to get these letters to you without possibly complicating things because I'm not supposed to see you ever again. But hand-delivery is the only option. I can't risk mailing it, and I can't just leave it on your porch. If someone intercepts this, it's all over for you.

It's been a month, Bennett. A month of biding my time and waiting for things to die down so that when I sneak to your house, no one will notice. But I can't wait anymore. I have to see you and apologize to your face, and if you won't speak to me, I'll just give you all this. The rest of our story.

Maybe you'll read it someday and understand.
Until then,

Madelyn

*

You're gone.

I went to your house and I knocked on the door and no one was there. I wanted to go back later. I thought that maybe your class hours were different in the new quarter and you were still on campus, or that maybe, if they really did fire you, you were working somewhere else now, teaching night classes, and you'd be home soon.

The thing was, the gate on your driveway had been shut when I'd arrived, which I figured meant you didn't want visitors. I'd parked near the road and then slipped through the gate to go to your house. After you didn't answer, I went back to my car and stood there, one hand on the door, reluctant to leave without seeing you, and your neighbor saw me.

And without so much as a hello, he said two words that shattered everything I'd hoped for:

"He moved."

I froze there on the gravel drive, the rain sprinkling down around me, darkening the surface, and said simply, "Huh?"

The guy, a little overweight with a goatee and a newsboy cap, shrugged. "Up and moved to Brooklyn or Baltimore or something. A big U-Haul arrived a couple weeks ago and I haven't seen him since."

"Well, which is it?"

He shrugged again and kept walking, up the little steps to his house.

"Wait! How do I find him?" I asked.

He turned around. "Dunno. Moved out in a real hurry. Sorry."

Then he pushed open his back door and slipped inside.

And that was it, Bennett.

I would never see you again.

*

I MISS YOU.

*

I DON'T LIKE being alone.

*

I'M SORRY. I'M sorry. I'm sorry I'm sorry. This hurts more than I expected.

Dear Bennett,

I've kept these pages for two years. Two long years. I haven't read them in months, but today everything changed.

Because I saw you today. December 13th, two years from that night at the cabin.

It's funny, because that first year after you left you were all I could think about, and this past year I've been trying so hard to move on that I somehow blocked it all.

But I guess my subconscious was thinking of you, because I was drawn to that mountain, to taking that once-familiar hike. And that's what brought us back together.

Your hair is shorter now, and when our eyes met for the first time in two years, the look you gave me was more guarded than joyous. But it was you, and my heart stopped so completely I felt as though the oxygen in my blood had disappeared, and I had to put a hand on a nearby tree to keep from falling to the ground.

That must sound melodramatic, but it's the truth. I thought I'd never see you again, and I'd resigned myself to that. It started with me handling it one day at a time—so much like climbing the mountain, one step a time.

I was standing at the top of Mt. Peak, my jacket zipped up to my chin to ward off the cold. I don't know why I hiked up there that day. The wintery air made my lungs hurt, but it was a good sort of pain.

I was staring down at the Enumclaw Plateau, the farmlands dotted with cows, my old high school stretched out in the distance, Mt. Rainier at my back. When I heard someone on the trail, I turned to look, just a glance, and then did a double take.

You. In one instant—that moment our eyes met—a swirl of memories spun around me, and the strongest image was of you that night in your cabin, that instant your eyes darkened to match the winter night.

You froze there, one foot on the top of the mountain, the other still on the trail, and stared back at me, and I wondered if you might spin around and bolt, or maybe stride right over and yell at me, really scream, say the things you must have thought these last two years.

Two years, Bennett. That makes me eighteen now. Legal. I don't expect that to matter anymore, but I do wonder if I even look different, if I think differently, if I *am* different. It's impossible not to wonder these things, because two years was supposed to mean everything.

I turned around and stared at you, and you took that last step, until you were standing at the top also. Like you planned to stay. We were dozens of feet apart, but neither of us moved or spoke, and the whole winter could have passed us by and I don't think I would have noticed, because to me the world had stopped turning.

"I'm sorry," I finally said. The two words I wanted you to hear more than any others. You could bolt in the next instant but you'd finally know that I was sorry, and that would be enough.

It would have to be enough.

Your jaw tensed but you nodded, and I waited for anger to swim into your eyes, but it didn't.

"I thought I'd never see you again," I said.

"My parents still live around here. I'm in town for the holidays," you said.

I nodded, finally taking a few steps closer to you. You didn't do the same, just crossed your arms.

"Where's Voldemort?"

You frowned, and your eyes turned sad around the edges. "Gone," you said. "He was thirteen. He didn't do so well this winter. It gets cold in Boston."

Boston. You moved to Boston. *Thousands* of miles because of me. "I'm sorry," I said again, this time for a different reason.

"Yeah. Me too." You sighed, deeply, a sigh about so much more than your dog. You kicked a rock and it skittered past me, hit a tree trunk, and tumbled down the mountainside. You didn't speak again until the quiet sounds of its descent fell silent. "Why'd you do it?"

I blinked, studying your face, trying to figure out if you wanted a real answer. I hadn't expected you to want to know, to give me enough time to explain. I'd expected just anger. Hurt. Betrayal. "I—"

But what could I say, where could I start? I wrote you hundreds of pages to try to explain. Even if the world *had* stopped and we'd had all the time we wanted, I didn't think I could have said the right things. "Does it matter?"

"Yes," you said, zipping your jacket all the way up. "No." You paused. "I don't know. "

That was how I felt, too. Yes, no, I don't know. Round and around.

"I wrote it all down," I said. "All the ways I lied to you. I was going to send it to the police station to try and get you released, but then I found out you hadn't really been arrested."

"Oh."

I closed my eyes and willed the words to appear, to magically transform from a tangle of excuses into something real. I wanted a lot of things for myself, but mostly I wanted things to be okay with you, I wanted the knowledge that what I'd done hadn't devastated you in every way possible.

"You ruined me," you said, and my eyes popped open, darted up to meet yours, shocked that you'd spoken the words I'd been so terrified to hear. And the worst part of it all is that your words weren't an accusation—they were the simple truth. I'd stolen everything.

"I know." I tangle both hands in my hair as if I want to rip it all out, but then I let go and my arms fall to my sides again. "I know," I said again. "You lost your job and you moved away and it was because of me."

You nodded, accepting this simple fact. Then you shook your head. "No, actually, they didn't fire me. I quit. I'm sure I would have been fired if they'd launched an investigation. But I wasn't charged with anything, and the quarter was over, so I just moved. Right away. I don't know what would have happened if I'd stayed. I didn't teach for a while, but then I got a job with an online university. I like it more than I thought I would."

I didn't know what you were saying—if you meant you forgave me, or hated me, or what—but I just stood there, breathless.

"I'm engaged," you added. And what followed, for me, was such a strange swirl of hurt and happiness. Because I'd spent the last two years thinking I'd destroyed everything, that you had no hope of a real future because of what I'd done, and now here you were, telling me you had one. A future.

"Oh." I raked in a shallow breath. "Congratulations."

"I told her about you."

I must have reacted visibly, betraying my shock, because the tiniest smile graced your lips, a sad sort of humor.

"Why?"

"Because I couldn't start our life together based on lies. She thought I'd moved to Boston because I preferred the east coast, when really I just wanted to be here. Teaching. I wanted to buy that house and live close to my parents and have the life I'd planned for. And she deserved to know who I was. What I'd done."

"What *I* did," I said.

You shook your head. "No, it was us."

Us. So maybe there is an us, even if it's only a footnote in your life.

You swallowed but didn't take your eyes off of me. "I almost lost her. Christ, I haven't been that scared in…" And then you broke eye contact and looked away. "In a couple of years."

"But you didn't," I say.

"No. I guess there's something to be said for honesty."

It wasn't an intentional barb, but it was one just the same, and I had to nod.

"So you're okay," I said, more of a statement then a question.

"Yeah. Boston's nice. The weather can be hell and the traffic is horrible, but I like living in a big city more than I expected to." You chewed on your lip, then looked up at me again. "And you?"

I pursed my lips and nodded. "Yeah, I'm okay." And I was. I really am okay, Bennett. Somehow, through it all, I've come back to myself. No, not back to myself the way I'd been—I actually *found* myself, the girl I would have been all along if I hadn't let other people's expectations smother me. "I mean, no boyfriend or anything, but I'm okay with that. I have time."

"Yeah. You do."

"I'm going to culinary school now. Just made it through the first quarter. My mom doesn't really get it, but she's a terrible cook anyway. Dad actually likes the idea. He's already volunteered as my official taste-tester. And he bought me all these ridiculously expensive pots and pans." I was silent for a second. "I'm excited, I guess. When I'm there, I forget everything else and just cook."

You nodded, and things went quiet again. It was hard to imagine the days we'd talked for hours, hard to imagine the connection we'd had when we were two strangers now. Somehow you'd become ... just ... someone that I used to know.

I'd given you something, a piece of me, something you'd always have.

But the rest of me ... I took it back.

"Well, take care of yourself, okay?" you said, edging back toward the trail.

"Wait!" I said, taking another step. "Do you want it?"

"What?"

"The letter. The one I wrote to you, to explain everything. To make you understand why I did what I did."

You stared into my eyes for a long, lingering moment, and I don't know what you were thinking. Because I didn't know you anymore. You'd grown and changed just like I had, and the people we were back then ... they didn't exist anymore.

But eventually, you shook your head. "No. I don't need it. You keep it."

I nodded, a lump growing in my throat. Maybe I didn't know you, but some part of me still felt gaping, still wanted to run to you and rest my cheek against your chest and close my eyes and remember how it felt to be together. Remember how on top of the world we were.

Before the world crashed down around us.

"Well ... good luck," you said. "I hope someday you find what you're looking for. Maybe someday I'll dine at one of your restaurants."

"Uh-hmm," I say, keeping my voice as even as possible. "And congratulations. I hope it lasts forever."

As much as it hurt to say that, I meant it. If I couldn't have you, if you weren't mine, you deserved to belong to someone.

You smiled then, a real smile, one that reminded me of the you I knew before it all went wrong. And something warm bloomed inside me as I realized I hadn't stolen that smile from you after all, that on the other side of the country another girl got to see that glow, bask in the warmth of it. "Yeah, me too."

And then you turned and left me standing on top of that mountain.

And now here I am, standing in the backyard writing this last letter, so that I can fold it in half and throw it into the fire pit next to the two hundred other pages, the ones already twisted and blackened, rising in the smoke and floating away. It's snowing today—something that only ever happens once or twice a year in Enumclaw—and the snowflakes scatter on my sleeves, melt in my hair, but I hardly notice them as I write this.

I guess it's a fitting send-off, that the night we spent together was one of snow, and in the last moment we share together, it's snowing too.

Because I'm letting go, Bennett. All the way. I've sifted through the letters from time to time, these past two years—tried to understand it all, tried to imagine where you'd ended up, how you felt about me, what it all really meant in the grand scheme of things.

But now I know you're okay, and somehow, I have to be okay too.

I'm letting go of the hurt and the sadness and the guilt, and most of all...

I'm letting go of you.

Acknowledgments

Many thanks to:

Bob Diforio, who is the kind of literary agent I can only hope to become—kind, tireless, and all-knowing.

Brian Farrey-Latz, for making me laugh at my own writing and for threatening me with cow jokes.

The rest of the Flux team, for turning my little manuscript into a real book. You guys are some of the best at what you do.

My friends on Twitter, who help me procrastinate on a daily basis.

Every reader who has ever sent me an email. You guys are amazing and make this whole thing worth it.

And finally, special thanks to Deputy Richtmeyer with the King County Sheriff's Office for not batting an eye at all my very specific questions, and for putting my mind at ease that I'll never be sucked out of an airplane if someone shoots a gun inside at an elevation of 30,000 feet. Research rocks.

About the Author

Amanda Grace is a pseudonym for Mandy Hubbard, author of *Prada & Prejudice* and *You Wish*, romantic comedies for teens. Her serious novels for teens, *But I Love Him* and *In Too Deep*, were released by Flux in 2011 and 2012. A cowgirl at heart, she enjoys riding horses and ATVs and singing horribly to the latest country tune. She's currently living happily ever after with her husband and daughter in Enumclaw, Washington.

Visit Mandy at amandagracebooks.blogspot.com, or follow her on Twitter @MandyHubbard.